Meet Me at Marmaris Castle
By Carla Kovach

Copyright

Disclaimer

Dedication

Many thanks to Nigel Buckley and Brooke Venables for all your help.

Leopard print shoes

I love the shoes. He will love the shoes, that's if he turns up. I hope he loves me more than the shoes but the shoes would be a start. Do I want him to love me? A decade is a long time and now I have stretch marks. I know people make promises but sometimes circumstances dictate whether a person is able to fulfil those promises. "Meet me at Marmaris Castle," he'd said. That was almost ten years ago. Had he since married like I had? Maybe he's divorced like me. I trembled at the thought. I don't have a plan if he doesn't show. I suppose at the very least I'll get a holiday. I haven't really had much time to myself since having the girls so a holiday sounds okay, just not as okay as seeing Jason again. I stare at the shoes, admiring the heel and the leopard print pattern, and I grin. He will definitely love the shoes. I pack them in my case, ready to fly the day after tomorrow. Take me to Marmaris.

Florida, the children and her

Phillip's car pulled up on time. I paused and watched as he opened 'her' car door. Oh no, does she have to get out? My heart feels as though it's pumping at the back of my throat, making me feel like I need to gag. She's getting out of the car. Yes, Miss younger, slimmer, and now just to top it off, pregnant, has just stepped out. Why is it that she looks like she's been kitted out in the best that John Lewis can offer? When I was pregnant with the twins, I had to make do with leggings and his oversized tee-shirts. Oh yes, my wide-fit trainers were really glamorous; bloody puffy ankles. That's how it goes when you're pregnant and a bit hard up. I checked my reflection as they walked up the path. Hair at its best – check, loving the honey hi-lights. Make-up, tidy if not slightly foxy – check. Clothes – best in my price range – check. You can't go wrong with jeans and a fitted shirt. The doorbell rang. The girls ran down the stairs. "Daddy," Emily shouted. Shelly followed closely, carrying her favourite teddy bear. I heard the door open.

"Hello my lovely ladies. Are you excited?" Phillip asked. The girls yelled at the same time.

At first I hadn't been pleased about him taking them to Florida with 'her.' It's a long way to go and I've never been apart from them for that long. Three weeks without their shrill voices and animated play was going to seem strange and then there's 'her.' Her has a name. Her is called Mallory. What kind of a name is Mallory? Mallory works in management. Mallory's American father is some sort of business tycoon, IT sector I think. Mallory obviously works for Daddy's company. Mallory has the shiniest hair and the firmest behind ever thanks to her personal trainer at the gym. Her gym has a steam room. I imagine her visiting the nutritionist just before getting her weekly manicure. My hands shake. I can see the attraction, I really can. Phillip and I did nothing but argue and Mallory has a fabulous house, a trim bottom and she has a swimming pool. I know this because my children come back from their country retreat and ask me why we can't have a swimming pool too. I have no idea why Mallory wanted to put my husband in that lovely house but hey, what Mallory seems to want, Mallory gets. It was no good delaying the inevitable. I had to face them.

I took a deep breath and walked down the stairs. Play it cool Annie. Take one step after another in the ridiculously high heels you've treated yourself to. Whatever you do, don't stumble. Be elegant, walk tall and show them that air of confidence that you've been practising so well. They come into view and I notice that they both look so well preened. Had Phillip gotten a fake tan? I tut. I have to stop doing that. I'm allowing parts of Mallory to enter my mind. Mallory says gotten all the time. The children even come home saying gotten. I'm forever correcting them.

Phillip smiled at me as he took Shelly's case from the hall. He'd had his teeth whitened. That had to be Mallory's influence.

"Hello Sweetie," Mallory said as she leaned in and kissed me on the cheek. I allowed her to hug me. "They are going to have such an awesome time. I don't want you to worry about them for a single moment. You know I have an Aunt Ellie living in Miami, we'll be staying at her beach house for one of the weeks. They will have such an amazing experience," she said. I inhaled her perfume. I didn't recognise the smell but it was no eau de toilette. It had a depth and a sweetness, which left me needing to inhale again. Her clothes felt soft to the touch. There was no colour fading or bobbling on her light shawl. It was then I realised that the size twelve high street jeans that were holding in my size fourteen stomach had nothing on her. I'll get my own back when she reaches the third trimester.

Emily left the house and began walking down the path. "Do I get a hug Emily," I called. She giggled and ran back.

"Sorry Mummy," she said as she threw her arms around my waist. I kneeled and kissed her soft cheek.

"I think they're just so excited to go and see Micky and Minnie, aren't you girls?" Mallory shouted.

The twins yelled again. Big grins spread across their faces. "Even Ernie is looking forward to it," Emily said as she held up her scruffy teddy bear, the bear that Phillip and I had given her on her first birthday. The girls still looked so tiny. My heart missed a beat at the thought of them leaving me for a whole three weeks but despite our previous differences, Phillip is an excellent father. I just hoped in the meantime that Emily and Shelly would still think I was a good mother, after all, buying that swimming pool will never be on the cards.

"Mummy, I forgot Bertie," Shelly said as she hugged me. Bertie is Emily's first birthday bear. My girls rarely go anywhere without their special bears.

"That's okay Love. I'll go and get Bertie for you," I said as I left her at the door and ran up the stairs. I ran into their room and started lifting the bedding and opening the cupboards. Bertie was nowhere to be seen. I've never known anything else get so lost, so many times. Shelly certainly was the forgetful one. I paced up and down as I tried to think back. She'd had Bertie at breakfast and then she'd taken Bertie upstairs when she was getting dressed.

"We have to get going soon. Can you hurry up?" Phillip called.

"I'm trying," I said. I heard him murmuring to Mallory. The girls were giggling and running around on the drive, no doubt excited to be going to Disney World. I kneeled down and looked under the bed. How had Bertie ended up there, flush against the wall? I fell onto my front and reached as far as I could. I touched the bear's arm. Just a bit further and I'd have the bear in my hand. I reached again and managed to grab it. "Ouch," I yelled as I went to kneel up. My hair was stuck in a bed spring.

"Annie. I'm real sorry to hurry you but we have a flight to catch," Mallory said.

I wrenched my hair from the spring and yelped as a few strands ripped out. Gripping Bertie, I hurried along the landing and ran down the stairs. That's when time stopped; that's how it seemed anyway. Halfway down, I missed the step in my ridiculous shoes. No longer did I feel hot, I felt steaming, stuffy, rushed and flustered. I remember slinging the bear and grabbing the bannister. I remember Phillip and Mallory staring at me as I slid on my bum, hair everywhere, arms flaying, grabbing anything. Then, I landed with my legs apart at the bottom of the stairs. Keep smiling, I thought. Don't let them see your pain. As I went to stand, the top button on my jeans pinged and hit the front door, allowing my stomach to escape over my waistband.

"Are you okay Sweetie?" Mallory said as she ran over to me.

"I'm fine," I replied, smiling as I tried to rake my fingers through my hair.

"Here, don't try to lift her in your condition," Phillip called as he ran over and offered me a hand up. The cheek of it. How heavy did he think I was? Did he think I would break little Mallory?

"I said I'm fine." I grabbed the bannister and pulled myself up. My arm ached at the socket and my rear felt as though I'd taken a kicking but I wouldn't show them my pain. "See, no damage done," I said as I gasped for breath and placed a mass of tangled hair behind my ear.

The girls were still running around in the garden. Phillip bent down and picked Bertie up. Shelly ran up to him and he passed her the bear. "Thank you Daddy." Thank Daddy why don't you. I wanted to cry but I knew that would be silly. It wasn't Shelly's fault I'd fallen down the stars while trying to reunite her with her bear.

Phillip looked up at me and said, "Mummy found the bear." At least he had some decency in there.

Mallory touched him on the arm, displaying her fiery red nails. "We have to go, really. Girls, say goodbye to your Mummy."

Shelly and Emily ran up to me. I hugged them both at the same time. My girls were going away with their dad, without me, for the first time. I was going away without them for the first time since I'd had them too. I felt a tear welling up in the corner of my eye. Mallory looked at me. "We'll take real good care of them, really we will," she said as she hugged me. I hugged her back.

Phillip and Mallory have been together for two years. He had cheated on me with her, but we hadn't been happy. I'd known for a long time he wasn't the one but we'd planned to have a baby anyway. Foolish, I know, but neither of us were getting younger and we both saw children as being a part of our future. That baby had ended up being two babies. We made a go of it and it hadn't worked. Our lack of love wasn't Mallory's fault. Her timing sucked but it wasn't her fault. I felt like hitting myself for using another one of her words. Since when had I ever used the word sucked apart from in past tense when referring to how one consumed a popsicle? I blushed, there were other times. Anyway, moving on swiftly, I could slap myself again. It's an ice-lolly. Why did the girls keep bringing these damn words home?

I watched as they all got in the car and buckled up. I waved to the girls. The car left the street and they were gone. A tear trickled down my face. I promised myself I wouldn't cry and look at me now. I sobbed in the doorway, smearing all the make-up I'd spent ages applying. I closed the door and grabbed my phone from the side. What does a woman do when she's sobbing her heart out like a baby? She calls her best friend and has a good natter. "Beverley, can you talk?" I said as I bawled down the phone.

Up the buff

Children in flight, due to arrive in Florida this evening. Bags packed. Advanced Passenger Information completed. Passport, insurance, hotel and travel documents – all in the envelope on top of the case. I opened the envelope just to make sure. I'd opened it three times and three times I'd confirmed that I had everything. Taxi booked. Cash exchanged. Bikini packed – yes, I have a bikini for the first time since giving birth.

With several hours to spare, I needed to get beach buff and my friend Beverley took great delight in telling me that this begins with a bikini wax. Beverley thinks that as soon as I see him, we'll jump into bed together, have the wildest night I've ever had in my life and then I'll get over this historical, holiday-guy, obsession. I keep reminding her that it was ten years ago and anything could've happened. Deep down, I'm pretty sure, all the flattery he'd bestowed upon me was empty talk after a few Brandy Alexanders, and a smoking hot two-day fling. I keep telling her he won't turn up and that's okay by me. I have three hundred books on my Kindle and I'm looking forward to a bit of me time. Lying on a beach, reading, eating ice-cream and drinking cocktails, sounds perfect to me; man or no man.

I remember Beverley giving me a confused look after I told her I'd had this fling. It had been obvious by her sniggering that she'd never imagined me to be the holiday fling type, and she was right. What happened with Jason was a one off, totally out of character.

Beverley and I work in a school together. I teach reception class, she is the bursar. We meet for coffee on the high street every other Saturday. I wear cardies, in fact, I have one for every day of the week. The children adore the bright coloured ones. For my forty-fifth birthday, Beverley and the other staff surprised me with a cake in the shape of a cardigan. That's why Beverley gave me the look when I mentioned my fling. I haven't even had a date since my divorce. Beverley had never seen me as the type of person to have a wild moment. If

I'm honest I can barely believe that 'Annie the holiday fling bandit' ever existed. I'm not hip, I'm not cool, and I haven't entered a nightclub in at least fifteen years, except for that one time with Jason, in Marmaris. As a rule, I don't like clubs but I liked being with Jason. I'd have followed Jason anywhere.

Last week, when Beverley and I met for our regular coffee, she said I needed to 'up the buff.' She has a way of saying things with a dirty little snigger. I tried to explain that my child bearing days were behind me but she just laughed. "The buff," she repeated, elongating every letter. That's when she took me shopping and turned me into the foxy, heel wearing, slick-haired siren that I am today. Beverley said the kitten heels were too small and the killer heels would be a dead cert in the bedroom department. How many times did I have to tell her? I didn't anticipate that the bedroom department was going to happen. But I agreed with her on her shoe choice, maybe part of me was hopeful. My safe wardrobe was no good for Marmaris. I purchased both the killer and the kitten heels. I needed summer dresses, shorts and vest tops. I'd endured her diet plan of grapefruit, coffee, cabbage soup and some mystery powder you dissolve in water, made from seaweed I think. To her credit, I'd been grumpy for several weeks, but I'd lost a whole eighteen pounds and now I felt epic, at least I had until she insisted I was wearing a bikini. "But I have a baby belly," I remember yelling at her. She passed me a fifties style, sailor girl, pin-up bikini and pushed me into the dressing room. Beverley was right. New hairdo in honey tones, a light tanning cream, the perfect fitting bikini; I'd been underestimating my siren powers all these years, hiding safely under my chunky knitwear. Beverley did try to get me to ditch the knitwear. We argued for a whole ten minutes but I won the battle. My trusty knitwear remains hanging up in the wardrobe, ready for my return.

The doorbell rang, dragging me back to reality. Where was I? Bikini wax. Why had I agreed to this? I have razors and soap. Why go through the indignity of revealing your barely concealed lady bits to some young thing whose aim is to attack you with hot wax and tweezers? The tweezers are for my eyebrows by the way. As far as I'm aware, my landing strip, as Beverley calls it, will not be achieved by using tweezers, thank goodness. I opened the door. "Right, I suppose there's no getting out of this," I said as I left the house and pulled the door closed.

"Not if you want to up the buff. Have I been right so far in everything that I've helped you with?" As always, she looked foxy. Tight leggings and peep-toe shoes were her casual wardrobe staples. Considering she was fifty-two and a few years older than me, she always looked younger and definitely turned more heads. She had what I'd consider to be a balanced core. She could bend and stretch with ease, maybe it was down to her weekly yoga sessions. If I did too much bending and stretching, tendons were likely to snap. I admired her confidence. She regularly attended a few dates per month through various dating sites. She's my inspiration. If I had the energy, I'd choose to be more like Beverley. Since becoming best friends with her after my divorce, I'm almost a changed woman. I nodded, smiled, and got in her car, ready for my complete Beverley inspired transformation.

I stared out of the car window, wondering where the past ten years had gone. My girls had been my entire life for the past four years and playing house with Phillip had zapped away the years previous to that. Having them had changed me in ways I'd never imagined. Two little ones who were constantly full of energy had drained me to the point of exhaustion. I love them more than anything, but I'd let myself go. When I found out they were going to Florida, that special date rang in my head. I could make the date. I could meet Jason at Marmaris Castle or should I say, I could get myself to Marmaris Castle, alone, and see if he turned up.

I'd thought about Jason many times over the years. I'd imagined what my life would've been like if we'd have swapped numbers instead of making silly drunken small talk. I hadn't wanted to appear too desperate. I wanted him to ask for my number, but he never did. I hadn't told him where I lived or worked and he hadn't told me anything either. I wonder if he'd thought about me as many times as I had him. As I'd stepped on the coach to leave for the airport all those years ago, I remember him running up to the window. I opened it and he shouted. "Meet me at Marmaris Castle, this date, ten years from now. Seven in the evening, I'll be there," he'd called as the coach pulled off. I should've asked the driver to pull over and then I should've taken a taxi to the airport after speaking to him, but I remained seated and the coach left. I remember watching him getting smaller and smaller as the coach continued down the main run of Marmaris, leaving him and the hotel I'd been staying at in the distance. I remember my heart pounding and wanting to cry. We'd had a fantastic two days but was two days enough to really get to know someone? I may not have known him well, but I do know that a day hasn't passed without those words ringing through my head. "Meet me at Marmaris Castle."

"Did you hear me?"

"Sorry Bev, I was in a world of my own."

"Wendy's Waxing Salon awaits your arrival," she said as she got out of the car. "I think if I was meeting some lover guy in paradise, I'd be in my own world."

I smiled and followed her through the door, to my doom. "You know Bev, I'm fairly tidy down there. I don't think I really need to do this-"

Beverley placed her hand over my mouth. "Shhh. Trust me Annie. This is for your own good." I said no more. Beverley knew best as she'd pointed out several times. She'd been right so far.

Okay. Think of England. Think of what happened in Coronation Street last night. Think of the beach, think of handsome Jason. Think of anything but not the woman who, at times, has a fairly good view of my vagina. I closed my eyes while Wendy prepped me.

As Beverley reminded me, I'd had smear tests and given birth, there's nothing to be embarrassed about. I felt the wax being spread on my nether regions. I clenched my teeth. All thoughts had left my mind except for the impending strip being pulled away. I flinched. A few more times and it was over. Just brows, nails, and toes to go, but first coffee. As far as I'm concerned coffee fixes anything, even an itchy, hot, sore vagina.

*****

"That wasn't so bad was it? I always have one before I go on my hols," Beverley said as she sipped her mocha. Although her odd diet was extreme, she always let herself off when it came to sugar laden fancy coffees. We both did. It was the start of my holiday and I wanted a raspberry mocha frappe more than anything. I'd go as far as saying, after the torturous morning I'd had, I deserved one. It's not every day you fall down the stairs in front of your ex-husbands younger, slimmer girlfriend and it's not every day you get some woman ripping hairs from your private parts, leaving you with what could be termed as mild and embarrassing discomfort. I just hope the gel manicure is easier.

"Bottoms up," Beverley said as she dunked a little chocolate biscuit in her mocha.

I smiled. If nothing else, Beverley and I had become really close friends. She'd renewed my confidence in myself which in itself was invaluable. For Heaven's sake! I was going on holiday alone. I'd revamped my body, mind and wardrobe for this moment and I had Beverley to thank.

"Thanks for being such a good friend Bev," I said as I slurped my frappe. She smiled then leaned over as she took a sip of her drink. A wisp of hair escaped from her clip and brushed the foamy cocoa that was stuck around the insides of her cup. She lifted the hair out, placed the brown curl in her mouth and licked off the froth. "Elegant as usual," I said as she gazed over my shoulder. I turned. A man who looked to be in his late thirties was already eyeing her up. "You big flirt," I whispered as I kicked her under the table. We both laughed. I'd miss Beverley. We arranged to catch up as soon as I returned. I left her in the coffee shop twiddling her hair and smiling at the man.

Flying solo with the exception of wine

Arrived at Birmingham International Airport safely -
check. Tipped the taxi driver - check. Cases checked in -
check. It's just me and my hand luggage until I arrive at
Dalaman. I wandered through the duty free shop and
picked up a sample perfume. I've never been one to turn
down a free squirt. Nice, elements of ylang-ylang. Why
were my hands shaking? I placed the bottle back down,
walked through to the lounge and spotted the bar at the
other end of the room. A large wine might be just what I
need to calm the nerves.

I'm not normally scared of flying. I'd travelled a
lot during my twenties, venturing around the USA and
Europe by car, with friends and alone. I looked down at
my hands and realised that over recent years I'd lost a

piece of myself. Most of my friends are settled. Their children are in their teens or almost grown up. I still have little ones. It's not like I didn't want a family earlier, I just never found the right person. I suppose I gave up trying in the end and settled for Phillip. In a way, he was my last option to have the family I craved. For that I would always give Phillip my gratitude. A tear trickled down my cheek. Maybe it was me who hadn't make enough effort. When he'd met me, I'd been independent, opinionated and fun to be around. He'd never had children either. Maybe he'd seen me as his last chance too. I mean, he had no idea Mallory was going to come along. I have no idea what she sees in him. I'm not jealous, really I'm not, they're just such a mismatched pair. Maybe that's the secret to happiness. Maybe I slowly morphed into Phillip while I was with him. Maybe all he could see was a reflection of himself when he looked into my eyes. He soon changed. He wanted trendier clothes and he wanted to go out. I did too but I was always the one looking after the girls. He'd think it was okay to leave me all the time with the twins while he continued his life as if we'd never had them. I can see it now. He'd felt trapped. I know because I'd felt trapped. Saying that doesn't mean that I don't love my children, it means they change your life. The change is so big; I imagine any person is seldom prepared for what's to come.

I thought of Mallory. Ultimately she stole Phillip from me or should I say I gave him to her. I didn't really make any effort to keep him. I know full well he'd have told her that we were virtually over. He wouldn't have been wrong. He'd been sleeping on the settee for the past year and we'd not been intimate. We tried once but it had felt awkward. All the wine in the world wouldn't have fixed the gaping hole that was missing in our marriage. When he said he was leaving I was almost pleased. I think of Mallory as I hope the same doesn't happen to her when she has the baby. I hope he makes more of an effort with her than he did with me. I hope he becomes more hands-on than he was with our girls and in turn she wants to keep him around. Mallory is good with the girls and for that reason, she's good with me. Okay, maybe I am just a little jealous. I really wish I had her behind.

"Large red please," I said to the barman as I held out a note. He poured the wine and placed it in front of me. I put my bag on the only empty table in the bar area and sank into the chair. A couple with three children were just getting up and leaving the table next to me. Their little girl returned my smile as she walked away. I have this dilemma. I'm really glad to have a little time away from my girls. There's no doubt, they're hard work but I feel guilty that I'm not missing them as much as I should be. Should I feel bad about enjoying this time? Beverley had told me not to be silly, that one day they'll be grown up and I'll be glad I've managed to do some things just for me. Again, Beverley was right. I swigged the wine and felt its power travelling through my body.

Several men gathered around the vacant table next to me. I took another gulp of wine and grimaced. It wasn't the best of reds. Maybe I should've had something lighter like a vodka and coke. Condoms! I realised I hadn't thought about contraception for God knows how many years. Again, I reiterate, I have no intention of sleeping with him but what if? I can't go ill prepared for what might happen. Imagine having to come home and tell my mother I'm pregnant and be made to feel like some naive teenager. I'd been married when I'd had the girls, they were planned and I was forty-one, she still made me feel like I was a naughty girl. I gazed around. The bar area was full and I didn't want to lose my seat. "Could you watch my chair please while I just nip to the shop?" I asked one of the young men who was dressed in an 'Andy's Stag Do,' tee-shirt.

The group of lads slammed the empty glasses on the table and roared with laughter. "No worries. I'll save it for you," he replied as he put his feet on the chair and smiled.

I swigged the rest of my wine, grabbed my bag and headed towards the chemist. I found the correct aisle and began scanning my options. Orange flavour, ribbed green ones, sensitive, tickler. Whatever happened to normal? Where were the normal looking condoms? You know, the translucent things in standard packaging. A couple of girls walked by and stopped. A man with two young children was standing next to me. I stared up at an electric shaver, pretending to be interested in its functions. Please go, man with children. Please take your kids and let me buy my condoms in peace. I felt my face redden. I'm in my forties, a mother, a woman of the world and I'm burning up at the thought of buying a packet of condoms. The man turns to go. Now's my chance. I grab a pack. I have no idea what flavour or texture they are. Another man bumps into me.

"Ha ha. Lady on the red wine, saving chairs in bars," he said as he held his hand out to shake mine. I notice he's wearing an 'Andy's Stag Do,' tee-shirt.

"Andy's friend," I replied as I held out my strawberry extra thin condoms in my hand. What the hell have I just done?

"Andy's dad actually. I'm flattered that you thought I might be Andy's friend though. You have interesting taste in rubbers Red Wine Lady," he replied.

"They're not mine." I gulped as I threw the condoms back on the shelf.

Andy's dad grabbed several packets of red ticklers. "I recommend these, trust me," he said as he handed me a pack. I felt a burning sensation creeping up my neck and face as I reached out and took the packet off him with my trembling fingers.

"Thank you, for the recommendation. I mean, I just wanted them to swallow my drugs in and I thought strawberry flavour would taste nicer," I replied. What had I just said? I could've kicked myself.

He burst out laughing. I remained still, unsure as to whether I might faint, fall or vomit on him. "You're funny. If you're on your own, why don't you join us for a drink before you fly?"

I took a deep breath and held onto the shelf. Compose yourself Annie. The guy is just being nice. I look like a lone traveller, I look nervous and he's simply being kind.

"Anyway, we've taken your chair hostage. You'll have to sit with us. I'll leave you to purchase your red ticklers in peace shall I?" he said as he walked towards the tills. Standing on tiptoes, I peered over the shelf and watched as he paid for his condoms and left the shop. I exhaled and stared at the box in my hand. Red Ticklers. Would younger Annie have purchased the red ticklers? I agreed that she would have, especially after a glass of wine. I made my way to the till and to my surprise the shop assistant didn't look up once. As I left with my ticklers, my hands were shaking, not from nerves but exhilaration.

"Red Wine Lady," Andy's dad called, "we've got you a fresh one in." I noticed the boxes of condoms on the table. Andy's friends grabbed them and placed them in their hand luggage.

The lad who was saving my seat moved his feet off the chair as I approached. "Thank you," I replied.

"Where you heading today?" Andy's dad asked.

"Marmaris, oh and thanks for the drink," I said as I sipped the wine.

"Woo-hoo. Same flight, same resort. What's your name? If I bump into you, I can't keep calling you Red Wine Lady?"

"Annie. I can't keep calling you Andy's Dad either."

"Call me Gavin then. Nice to meet you Annie. Welcome to the party." I heard the call for our flight. The group downed the rest of their drinks and grabbed their bags. "Come on then Annie. Drink up," he said as he picked my bag up, waited for me to stand and then placed it over my shoulder. "Your perfume's lovely by the way."

I wish I could remember what it was called. I should've bought a bottle. Jason would've liked it, I'm sure. "Thank you," I replied, smiling.

*****

The flight had been a good one until about three hours in. Gavin's party were sitting by me which I was thankful for. Gavin had kept me amused with his witty life stories. Two marriages and one son, Andy, who was marrying the lovely Angela in a month. Gavin had worked as an architect in Birmingham for the past twenty years. He'd treated me to two more glasses of wine. They're only small bottles, I'd reasoned, but I was beginning to feel a little tipsy. Gavin continued to chat but my head started swimming. The seatbelt sign came on and the plane took a dip. I held my head, disorientated by the shaking and dipping. "It's only a bit of turbulence," Gavin said as he placed a friendly hand over my shoulder. The plane shook again. I felt the wine sloshing in my stomach. I reached into the pocket in front of my chair, grabbed the sick bag and vomited.

"Annie can't hold her wine," shouted one of Andy's friends, the one wearing the plastic wacky glasses.

"It's the turbulence," I said as I held the bag and called for attention. No one rushed over to attend to me.

"Better now?" Gavin asked. I nodded. The seatbelt sign went off. I stood and staggered to the toilet before anyone else could get there. I needed to dispose of my sick bag. Everyone was looking at me. I saw the man with the children, who I'd been standing next to in the shop when I'd been trying to buy condoms. He was shaking his head, telling his children how bad drinking was and to look at the silly lady who's drank so much she's made herself sick. Not for the first time today, I felt myself blushing. Yesterday, I was a respectable primary school teacher, today I'm a tipsy idiot doing the march of shame up a plane aisle, in turbulence, while holding a sick bag.

I had a wash and walked back to my seat, making a huge effort not to make eye contact with anyone.

"You okay Annie?" Gavin asked.

"I'm fine. Just tired and a little cold," I replied. There's only one thing I hated more than being sick and that was being sick in front of an audience. I needed a sleep. A quick hour would see me right. I closed my eyes then I felt someone placing something over me. I opened one eye and noticed that Gavin had placed his jacket over my lap.

"I owe you one Gavin. Drinks on me when I bump into you guys in Marmaris. I think I'll stick to coffee though," I mumbled as I fell into a light sleep.

That's not what it said in the brochure

The coach pulled up outside a small apartment block on the main road running through Marmaris. I guessed at it being about a fifteen-minute walk to the marina, in flip-flops. Ten years ago, I'd stayed at a Platinum hotel, only the best back then. I'd had a taxi transfer and a sea view. This time around, I'd booked a cheap deal which meant a bed, a bathroom and basic cooking facilities. Back then I had spare cash. I'd been buying a studio apartment just outside Birmingham and I rode a moped called Maurice. My cheap life choices had enabled me to be choosy when I travelled. Now, I had to keep a roof over the heads of my two children and the saloon car had soon followed, along with all the costs of maintaining it. It didn't take me long to realise that you can never have enough money when bringing up children. "Is this where you're staying?" Gavin asked.

"I hope not." I gazed up at the tired block above a row of shops. Maybe it'll look better in the morning.

"Ms Henderson," the rep called out.

"Looks like it is," I stood and grabbed my bag.

"See you around Annie Henderson. I'll hold you to that drink if we bump into each other." I looked at my watch, it was two-thirty in the morning. The transfer had taken over three hours. Gavin said they'd stopped at some castle like building for a toilet break but I'd slept through it. I rubbed my stiff neck as I stepped off the coach. The driver had already dragged my case from the hold. "Wait," I heard someone call.

"Jason," I said as I turned. I have no idea why I thought Jason would be there at that moment. Maybe it was wishful thinking combined with my guilt at not getting off the coach all those years ago.

"You really are half asleep," Gavin said as he laughed. "You've still got my jacket."

He was right. I'd put his jacket on during the flight and kept it on throughout the journey. Boy it was hot. I had no idea how I could've kept his jacket on for this long. The power of tiredness and air conditioning I suppose. I removed the jacket and handed it to him. "I'm so sorry, and I'm sorry I was ill on the plane. It can't have been pleasant sitting next to me," I said.

"It passed the time and the look on your face was rather amusing. I'm sure I'll see worse sights with this lot over the next few days. Anyway, take care Annie. I hope Bates Motel treats you okay," he replied as he turned to walk away.

"Sir, are you getting on the coach?" the driver asked as he started the engine up. Gavin stepped on the coach and it soon pulled away.

As I entered the hotel reception, a young man turned away from the film he was watching. "Can I help you?"

"Annie Henderson." I placed my booking details in front of him. The tired white-washed reception led to a tired staircase.

"The lift isn't working at the moment. We have engineer coming in one week," the man said in broken English. Great. I wasn't going to be using the lift during my holiday. I followed him up six flights of stairs, passing two flickering lights before we reached the loft room. "This is your room. To open the door, you need to hold like this." He lifted the door by the handle and swiftly placed the key in the lock. He wiggled if for a couple of minutes and then slammed into the door with his shoulder. "Don't be worried about hitting it," he said as he dragged my case into the room. He left, not even expecting a tip.

I turned the bathroom light on and heard a scurrying insect running away. I spotted it vanishing through a gap in the tiles. Sure a wash would make me feel more human, I turned the tap. Water burst out, splashing my face and top. Excellent, dodgy plumbing. I dried my face and walked back into the room. I can't believe that the brochure writers had the nerve to describe the small worktop and empty cupboard as a kitchenette. The table top fridge whirred and the cups on the tree were chipped. I swept a small pile of sugar off the worktop into my hand and threw it in the bin.

The door at the other end of the room led to a balcony. I already knew that this would give me a view of the road. Sweat began to drip down my face. I pressed the switch on the air conditioning unit. At least something was going right, the air con worked. I spread out on the bed and enjoyed the cool air blowing on my body.

My thoughts turned to my girls. I imagined them in one of the Disney resorts, having their photos taken with Snow White. I bet Phillip wouldn't take Mallory to a hotel like this one. Ahh, I hated myself for being so resentful. He did pay me maintenance but by the time the kids had attended their dance lessons, been to swimming club and done all the other day to day things that cost money, it was soon gone. I mentally totted up all the money I'd spent on waxing and clothes and felt my stomach tighten. I'd been totally selfish. I wish Beverley was here to make me feel better about myself. I picked up my phone and tried to find a Wi-Fi signal. The online brochure that I'd selected these apartments through had made a feature of the open Wi-Fi throughout the building. There were no open networks. I threw the phone on the bedside table. It was too late to send Beverley a Facebook message anyway. The only thing worth doing at this moment was sleeping. I'm sure even Bates Motel would look good when the sun was shining on it.

I closed my eyes and thought of Jason. It was the fifth of August tomorrow, the day I would be seeing Jason again. My mind flashed back to the first day I'd met him. My friend had deserted me. Well deserted isn't the best word. We'd booked the holiday together but she'd got a new job. The job had a training period attached to it, one where the dates were not negotiable. It was then just me. I decided that I'd still take the holiday even though I'd be alone. I'd never been to Turkey and many of my friends had said what great holidays they'd had there. Good old independent me didn't think twice about getting on that plane.

Five days I'd been on holiday, then I'd spotted the new arrival in the hotel next door. He seemed to be alone. I'd peered through the bushes that separated our complexes and he'd spotted me too. I remember his smile as he beckoned me to join him for a drink. This man was Jason. I remember thinking, what a coincidence, as his friend had also booked to go with him but couldn't make it. We'd eaten lunch together that day and before I knew it, he was rubbing sunscreen on my back. I hadn't been in a relationship for over five years and I hate to admit that I wanted him all over me before I'd even got to know him properly. Every time he'd rubbed sunscreen on my back, I'd been crazy with desire. I remember his brown floppy hair, his neatly fitted shirts and his wicked sense of humour, especially after a few drinks. He probably remembers my initial awkwardness. I'd tried to reciprocate with the sunscreen by holding the bottle over his back and the lid came off, covering him. He'd laughed but I'd been mortified. I smiled as I re-lived our time together in my mind. It had all worked out in the end once my nerves had calmed down. The fridge burst into a piercing whirring frenzy before stopping altogether. Maybe now was a good time to try and get some sleep.

I yawned and flicked the lamp off. I slipped out of my jeans and climbed under the sheet. What was tickling my toe? I leaped out of bed and turned on the light. Panting and sweating, I grabbed the television instructions from the side and remained poised to pounce on whatever was in my bed. My heart hammered against my ribcage as I spied the beetle scurrying along the floor and out through a gap in the skirting board. These gaps were starting to unsettle me. They were more like doorways for pests. Was I ever going to sleep? Rubbing my aching head, I slipped back into bed and decided I had to go to sleep.

For two hours I stared at the moonlit ceiling as I listened to the cistern dripping. I so wished at this point that I'd spent a little more on my accommodation. I had a whole week of this to go. This would surely test me to my limits. Jason had better be worth all this effort. I must've nodded off eventually.

*****

"Annie," called Phillip. "What are you doing here?"

"I should ask you the same thing. Why are you at the castle? Where's Jason?" I asked.

Phillip walked down the cobbled steps, took my hands and leaned in to kiss me. I pushed him back and turned to walk away but Mallory stopped me. "I always knew you weren't cool about us, even though I've taken your kids to Disney and all," she said.

"Mummy, you ruined Disney for us," Shelly shouted.

"I haven't done anything Poppet. Why do you say that?" I asked as I bent down to her level.

"Will you just hold this bag for a minute?" Gavin asked as he passed me a bag that was over spilling with vomit. I moved my hands away from him, refusing the bag. I went to grab Shelly's hand but she'd gone. Instead, I was holding hands with a sobbing Mallory.

"Now look what you've done," Phillip shouted as he held Emily in his arms.

"I'm sorry. I didn't mean to upset you Mallory," I said. I had ruined everything. It was all my fault. I felt tears trickling down my face as I crouched on the step with my head in my hands. I caught a glimpse of my dirty overgrown toenails. I'd had them painted a light rose pink before coming away. What had happened since leaving home and arriving in Turkey?

"I knew you'd meet me at Marmaris Castle," Jason called. I'd recognise that voice anywhere. It had been occupying my mind since he said those words back then. I wiped the tears from my eyes and noticed that Jason's shadow, standing in front of me, began to fade, leaving a pile of beetles crawling over my filthy toes. I ran, screaming for help as the insects scurried up my legs, in my shorts, in my hair and up my nose.

"No," I yelled as I jerked up in bed. Daylight had broken. "What was going on in my head? I drew back the sheet, half expecting to see a swarm of beetles scurrying around but the bed was clean. Gasping, I stumbled over to the balcony and slid the door open. I checked my phone, still no Wi-Fi. I took a few deep breaths and enjoyed the morning sun.

My apartment may resemble the Bates Motel but it sure looks like paradise out there. Okay, I exaggerate a little. I've never even watched Bates Motel for a start. My view is of the road but it still has charm. Below me, people are setting up shop for the day. I see two men and a woman, placing a couple of fold-up chairs outside a shop. A lad passes with a tray of apple tea and passes it to them. Cars pass, bikes pass. I watch a family enter the hotel on the other side of the road to the right. It has shiny glass frontage. A man in a smart uniform takes their case off them as they reach the door. Make the best of it Annie, I tell myself. That's all you can do. Welcome to Marmaris and hello holiday.

Waiting, hoping and adjusting ill-fitting underwear

I'd spent the last hour sitting in a café overlooking the marina. I'd learned my lesson well after the previous day, sticking with soft drinks and coffee all afternoon. I sipped the last of my water and placed the glass on the table. "Hesap lütfen?" I asked the man who'd served me. It had been ten years and I'd still remembered how to ask for the bill. He nodded, smiled and walked into the café. I looked at my watch. Fifteen minutes to go and I'd head up the steps to my fate. Would he be waiting? Was he sitting in a bar or café like I was now? Was his heart crashing against his ribcage in the same way that mine was? Don't be silly, I told myself. I was getting so worked up. There was a huge chance he wasn't even going to show up. Nevertheless, I'd made my best effort. Matching undies of Beverley's choice – on and awkward. By awkward, I mean the pants keep riding up the crack of my bottom. Checking around, I notice that everyone else is otherwise occupied. The couple dining at the table behind me are too busy gazing into each other's eyes to notice anything. The waiter is still in the café. The man in front of me, who'd been riding the three wheeled tricycle full of groceries had delivered to the yacht and left. I leaned up and grabbed the stringy material from the insides of my bottom. "Your bill Madam," the waiter said as he placed a little dish containing the bill on the table.

I stared at him. He'd seen me fishing my underwear out of my bottom. Why Beverley? Oh why did you make me buy this underwear? I said it was the wrong shape. I also said I wasn't quite a twelve. I'm still in need of fourteens. My face flushed as I slowly lowered my body back into my seat. I forced a smile as I looked at the waiter. I fumbled in my bag for my purse and grabbed a note.

"Thank you," I said as I stood and walked off. I have no idea how much money I'd left. As he isn't chasing me, I assume it was more than enough to cover my two waters, one cola and a latte. I didn't catch his reaction, didn't want to. Just keep walking Annie and don't look back. As I reached the bend I glanced back at the table. The waiter was standing there smiling. He waved. I tottered around the corner. I bet Mallory would never be seen in public pulling string panties from the crack of her pert bottom. Mallory would use the word panties, I'm sure of that.

If only I hadn't shamed myself yet again, I could've walked straight up the steps from the marina side to the castle. Now I'd been caught, I had to walk around. As I passed the restaurants, waiters called me. "No thank you, maybe later, another time," were my three main responses. I felt like I'd been saying that all day. There are only so many coffees I can drink. There are only so many sandwiches and meals I can eat. I kept walking until I reached Bar Street. I remembered this street so well. It was the street where all the action had taken place.

Jason had brought me to one of these bars. I remember doing shots. I remember dancing with him in strobe lighting. I remember falling into a taxi, laughing like I'd never laughed in my entire life. I remember how he'd booked a hotel room close by, both of us afraid that our respective hotels wouldn't entertain a plus one or worse still, we'd endure dirty looks the morning after. Okay, I admit that only I was concerned about the looks we'd get at our hotels. He'd stopped the taxi beside a moderate looking hotel in Içmeler, set next to one of the canals. How we ended up in a village a few miles down the road, I had no idea. I remember giggling as he said we were Mr and Mrs Jones. The receptionist knew what we were up to. It had been so obvious. We hadn't cared though.

I looked at my watch. Still several minutes to go. I leaned on a wall opposite the bottom of the castle steps. I had no idea if he'd approach the castle from the Marina or from Bar Street. I put my sunglasses on and thought back to that night once again.

We'd stumbled into the hotel room. I remember us staggering and laughing all the way to the bed. I watched him as he struggled to unbutton his shirt, in the end I'd helped him. He peeled off my sticky clothes. We were both sticky. It had been hot and we'd been dancing all night and without any hesitation I dragged him onto me as we kissed. There was nothing awkward about that encounter. It had happened, it was quick for both of us and we repeated it again twice the following day. I shivered as I remember his warm hands rubbing my body. I've missed out on so much the past few years. Phillip and I had a love life before the girls but it lacked passion. It worked for us in a functional way and it was satisfying but I can honestly say he'd never made me feel electric. Jason had made me feel electric. He could've done anything he'd wanted with me. I did tell Beverley that I probably wouldn't be sleeping with him. Who the hell was I kidding?

I brushed the creases out of my short floral dress. I'd worn the smaller heels. I know Beverley said the kitten heels wouldn't do the trick but I couldn't do the killers. I didn't want to remove my shoes at any point only to reveal a load of strategically placed plasters or worse, seeping bloody blisters. I think the right decision was made. Sorry Beverley.

As I waited, I saw a man take a turn towards the castle. Brown hair – check. About five nine in height – check. Why is he checking behind him as he continues towards the steps? Weird. Does he think he's being followed? Maybe he's checking that I'm not behind him. "Ouch," I whispered. That damn bra was springing a wire now.

A group of loud revellers passed me. I looked away not wanting to draw attention to myself. I glanced at them as they passed. Gavin was with his son and the rest of the guys I'd met in the airport. "Red Wine Lady," one of them shouted. They'd spotted me.

"Join us if you want Annie," Gavin called.

I waved back. "Have a good one, I might see you later."

"You best do. I've remembered that drink you promised us," He waved back and entered a bar.

I checked my watch. Grief, I was now late. I tottered towards the castle. The cobbled steps leading up to the castle were deserted. Businesses either side were now closed. I tapped with each step. If he was up there waiting, he'd sure know I was coming." My heart began to pound in my chest. I slipped on a cobble, not because I wasn't being careful in these dinky heels but because my knees were knocking. The heat was beginning to rise up from my chest to my neck. I clenched my hands together as I took a few more steps and finally reached the entrance to the castle. Where was he? Man with brown hair of correct height, where did you go? I leaned against the wall and a cat brushed against my legs and began to meow. I crouched down and stroked its head. I'd been foolish thinking I was worth a ten year wait. That man probably wasn't even Jason.

I closed my eyes and thought back to our second day of romance and lust. His every touch had made me tingle. I remember, I'd just got ready to go out. My hair was neat, my make-up perfect and my stringy backed dress had taken an age to get on. One touch from him had rendered me messy again. I'd helped him to rip the dress off. I'd welcomed him unpinning the hair that had taken me forty-five minutes to style and I'd encouraged him to ruin the make-up, which was soon smeared all over him. I hadn't cared. I'd never wanted anyone so badly and I wanted him now. I wanted him to be here. The cat meowed and ran away. I'd even been deserted by the cat.

A tear streamed down my face. Maybe Andy's stag do would welcome me to the party as long as I didn't vomit on anyone. I'll take the path down the marina though, I need to clear my head. I don't think that waiter will remember me anymore. Hopefully he's busier, so weird, lone lady, fishing her pants out of her bum, will be a distant memory. Another tear began to well. Don't start crying Annie.

I began the steady walk down. As I turned the bend between a house and the castle wall, Jason walked towards me. "You came," I said in a croaky voice. I allowed a smile to spread across my face.

"I thought you weren't coming. I got here ten minutes ago but you weren't here."

"Fashionably late?" I said as I ran up to him and threw my arms around his neck. He hugged me tight.

"Ten years I've waited for you Aggie," he said.

"Annie," I replied. I can't believe he forgot my name. Not a day's gone by when I don't say his name in my head.

"Sorry Annie. I'm just so excited to see you. I can't believe it's been ten years, that's all. Shall we go back to your hotel?" He gave me a dirty smile and winked.

Fast moving or what? His hands ruffled the back of my hair and sent a shiver down my spine. He had the same touch, the same amount of pressure. There was undeniably some feelings still there. I reached up and stroked his hair. "Wait, what's happening?" A clump of his hair was tangled in my fingers and coming away. "I'm so sorry," I said as I held his hairpiece out. He still had hair, he was obviously just filling in a small patch on the back of his head. "You look better without the piece," I said with a smile. It endeared me to know he was having the same issues with fashion as I was. Me with my stringy pants and him with his hair piece.

He grabbed it off me and placed it in his pocket. "Who I am I trying to kid? I wanted to look the same as when we first met. I had no idea if you'd come. You look stunningly beautiful," he said.

I smiled and looked away. "Me too, I know I've changed a bit. A lot changes in ten years. I sense we have a lot of catching up to do. Can we go for a drink?"

He smiled and nodded. It would have been interesting to just jump into where we left off ten years ago but I didn't want to. I wanted the thrill of the chase first, even if it was going to be a fast chase. I wanted a little romance, a bit of wining and dining. Most of all I wanted to be rid of these awful pants. As I led him back to the marina, I had a quick tug of the stringy bit. That's better.

"I know a nice quiet restaurant just up here. We can go there and catch up on the last ten years," he said. I liked his shirt, not as much as the flowery ones I remember him wearing. I'm a bit disappointed he called me Aggie though.

Desire, nerves, and the eye of evil

I followed as he took my hand and led me down the uneven steps until we reached the marina. The waiter who'd spotted me adjusting my pants earlier was facing the other way, trying to get the attention of a group of people approaching his restaurant. Please don't turn around, I thought as I passed. I stumbled as I tried to keep up with Jason. I can't remember him being in this much of a rush the last time we were together. I glanced back. Thank goodness, the waiter never saw me. I don't know why I worry so much. It's not as if he's going to call out and ask me if I've managed to fix my knickers. As I turned, a man on a pushbike, holding a dog on a lead rode by, almost knocking me off my feet. I stepped forward, pushing my big toe into what little room there was in the corner of my shoe. For a second, I could've cried but I thought of Beverley. Beverley would tell me to remain composed and keep smiling, so I did. "Can we slow down a bit? We have all night. We don't have to rush."

"I'm so sorry. It's just, I'm excited to sit down with you and catch up on the missing years." I stopped and took my shoe off, allowing my toes to splay out. I'm now even more grateful that I didn't wear the killer heels. I watched as Jason checked his watch and looked around. Did he have somewhere else to be?

The statue of the children that I'd passed earlier that day was just ahead. I stared up at the little girl holding the mini windmill and thought of my girls. "Bear with me, I just need to sit for a minute." I hobbled towards the statue's wall and collapsed onto it. I massaged my toe before placing the shoe back on.

"We're nearly there. It's just a little further. I hope you don't mind me choosing. They do nice fish there," Jason said as he held his hand out and helped me back up, once again rushing me.

Fish? I'm not sure about fish. I took his hand and walked beside him. He seemed to have slowed down to my pace. Maybe he was nervous like me. Back to fish. I don't quite know how to tell him that I'm not keen on fish. Like my girls, I'm quite fond of a fish and chip takeaway on a Friday night after work, but any other fish, I'm not so sure. Maybe I can get away with a steak, or something a bit more to my liking. Just go with it Annie. Try something new. I've had a new makeover, I have new clothes and I have found my sense of self coming back. I gazed at the huge yachts as we walked and I wondered what type of people owned them. All I saw was rows and rows of millionaires' yachts, enjoying the nightlife that was oozing from the marina at night.

Jason's hand was getting hotter. As we linked fingers I felt mine sliding with his. I'm not sure I liked the feeling. It was a sticky night though, not dissimilar to the night we first went out together. I used my other hand to smooth my hair. It had become unbelievably frizzy since I'd arrived. There was nothing sleek about the untamed bush that was beginning to appear on my head.

We soon arrived at the end of the promenade just before the bridge. "Table for two," the waiter called. The front tables were taken. He led us further into the restaurant and seated us at a smaller table, then he handed us a couple of menus.

"Shall we go for two Brandy Alexanders for old time sake?" Jason asked.

I thought back to the flight and my experience of drinking too much. I hadn't really been out drinking in years which is why the wine had hit me so hard the other day. I was out of practice. I know Beverley would tell me to lighten up. What would it look like if I asked for diet cola? Not good I'm sure. "Brandy Alexander sounds good," I replied. Tonight I am a vixen. I feel great in the dress; the underwear looks okay-ish and it certainly is bedroom underwear. I wouldn't wear it to work but I felt confident that Jason would like it.

Beverley had reassured me that ruby red was my colour and it would complement the multi-tonal shades of honey in my hair.

As he smiled and placed the order I reached down the front of my dress and slid the under-wiring back into my bra. Now I was ready to enjoy our cosy chat. "Do you trust me to order your food?" he asked. "I ate here last night and had the most amazing food ever." My heart fluttered and I nodded. I had made it. Ten years I'd dreamed about this moment and now I was here. For ten years, I'd lived a life of second bests when it came to relationships. I was now pinning all my hopes on this one being the one, the real one. Okay his hair was a little thinner and he'd put on a few pounds but that made me want him more. I was larger than when we'd first met, I also had to dye my hair without fail every six weeks. I had two children now. I hope he likes children. "Great. I'm glad you're good with the sea bass," he said. Had I somehow agreed to eating fish?

The cocktails arrived. I sipped the strong coffee-brandy concoction and felt its warmth sliding down my gullet. Smiling, I leaned over and placed my hand over Jason's. "So, tell me about yourself." Did I really just say that? "I mean I've been looking forward to hearing about what you've been doing with your life." I couldn't say what I meant. I wanted to know if he'd missed me. I knew he desired me from the way he reacted to our meeting at the castle. He'd wanted to go back to the hotel there and then.

He grabbed my hand and leaned over the table towards me. He kissed me on the lips. I felt his tongue touch mine and his other hand brush my cheek. This is what I'd been dreaming of. He is what I've wanted all this time. "You talk too much Annie," he said as he released me. I felt his hand reach under the table and stroke my knee. I closed my eyes and allowed his fingers to reach a little further up my leg. I didn't want food, I wanted him right there and then. Why hadn't I agreed to go back to the hotel immediately when we'd met at the castle? I'd known Jason for years, okay not really for years in a continuous time sense, but he had been in my thoughts for years. As far as I was concerned we were wasting what precious time we had, sitting here, eating some fish I didn't want. It was me who'd wanted to be wined and dined first. Why had I been such a bag of nerves? At this point, I was grateful that the long table cloth was hiding my pleasure, it wasn't however hiding my flustered face. "Two seabass," the waiter said as he leaned over me and placed the monster down.

I took a deep breath and felt the warmth draining from my face. "It's got an eye," I said as I stared at the plate.

"It has another one if you flip it over," Jason replied as he picked up his cutlery and began to eat. "It's so good though Annie. You'll love it, trust me." I turned and watched the other diners. Everyone was happily eating the fish. People smiled, laughed, chugged wine and kissed. Not one of them stared at the fish the way I stared at the fish. I pushed my fork through the flaky white flesh and fluffed up a little sample on the end of my fork.

"Bottoms up," I whispered as I opened my mouth and took a bite. It wasn't so bad, in fact, it had a salty oiliness to it from the sauce. I gobbled a mouth full of rice to eliminate the fishy taste in my mouth. Was it bad? Was it good? I have no idea. I'll continue to drown it out with rice. I chewed and chewed but eventually, I knew I'd have to swallow. I took a gulp of my drink and swallowed quickly. I'd done it. One mouthful, successfully chewed and swallowed, just about another thirty to go.

The eye stared back. "After I got back from Marmaris ten years ago, I ended up working in Newcastle ……" I stared at the eye. Who leaves eyes in fish when they cook it or should I say who leaves the head on? Why would anyone want to stare at a fish head when eating their dinner? "Annie, are you even listening to me?"

"Sorry." I placed my knife and fork together on the plate.

"Aren't you hungry?"

"No. I ate earlier. I didn't know we'd be eating. It was lovely though. Don't let me stop you enjoying yours," I replied.

I watched as he tucked into the fish, leaving nothing but the head and a perfect line of bones. He placed his cutlery down and ordered a bottle of wine. "I hope red's okay."

"I'll just have a coke please," I said.

"Coke? That's not the Annie I remember," he said as he began to laugh. "The Annie I remember was lining up shots on the bar and drinking anything in sight."

I blushed. "Red wine makes me sick." I have no idea if it was just the wine that caused my embarrassment on the plane but the wine hadn't helped. I couldn't do wine, not for a while, especially red.

"White then?" he asked.

"Beer?" I can do a beer, I know I can.

"Two large Efes please," he called. I'm not sure about the large one though. We'll see.

I remember him mentioning something about Newcastle before I got distracted with my thoughts on how I was going to practice fish avoidance with a certain level of discretion. "You live in Newcastle now?"

"No. I went to work in Newcastle after we met, ten years ago. I met someone and had a child as you do but it didn't work. I'll start again. I have a son, I split up from his mother a year ago. Some things just don't work out. I never stopped thinking about you Annie. All this time, no one has ever compared," he said as he placed his hand under the table and stroked my bare knee. I wanted to grab him and hold him and tell him that I felt the same. I probably wouldn't tell him that every erotic fantasy I'd had involved him, but you never know. Maybe after the beer I might. The Annie of ten years ago would tell him.

"I feel the same. I have twin girls of four years old. Their dad is with someone else and he's expecting his third. Me, I devote all my time to them and my job." I paused and bit my lip, worried that I'd just sounded boring. "I didn't think you'd be here."

"I knew I'd be here."

I couldn't reply. I had wanted to be here but I was mostly here because the girls had gone away with their dad and Mallory, and I wanted to feel carefree again, even if it was just for a few days. When Phillip announced the dates of their Florida trip, I'd been ecstatic. I knew I'd miss the girls but I also knew that my ten year fantasy could become a reality once again. I'd immediately booked the flight to Marmaris and had been nervously counting the days down since.

Jason looked at his watch again. Would it be rude of me to ask if he was in a rush? I concluded it would so I kept my mouth shut. The waiter brought the bill over and left it on the table. I felt Jason's hand leave my knee as he fished around for his wallet in his pocket. I opened my purse and left fifty lira on the table, which was half of the bill and a little tip. "This is my treat," he said as he gave it me back.

"Don't be silly," I said as I put my money back on the table. He rolled his eyes and made up the rest of the bill.

"What now?" I asked.

He looked at his watch. "It's getting late. I should get you back to your hotel."

I looked at my watch for the first time that evening. It wasn't late at all; it was only ten, but I knew exactly what he meant. I swigged the rest of my beer.

As we walked past all the bars to the taxi rank, I barely took anything in. The yachts were a blur. I couldn't remember passing the statue of the children and I forgot about the waiter from the café I was sitting in earlier that evening. He opened the car door. I told the taxi driver where to go and watched as he sniggered. Did everyone know the apartments I was staying at were awful?

Jason shuffled closer to me and cupped my chin. He leaned in and kissed me. I reciprocated, wanting him more and more with every stroke and every kiss. I felt his chest against mine and his hand tickling my leg. I have no idea what the taxi driver thought, I was just thankful he didn't know me. Jason flinched as my bra wire sprang out and pinched his skin through his tee-shirt.

"Sorry," I said. He ignored the pain and continued to kiss me.

The taxi stopped but Jason continued to kiss me. "We're here," I managed to say.

We got out of the taxi. Jason leaned in towards the car window and started fumbling with his money to pay. I stared up at the apartments. Here I was in paradise, with the man I'd desired for years and I was bringing him to a dump. Maybe he'd take one look and whisk me off to his hotel. I wondered whether he'd booked a luxurious hotel this time. I brushed my fingers through my hair. The frizz had come back. Would he like me? I didn't have a baby belly last time, I'd been well fit. I'm not supple now, I'm not even fit. I'm wearing ill-fitting silly underwear and I have a mosquito bite on my left boob. What the hell was I thinking?

The taxi left and he walked over to me. He checked his watch again. "In a rush are we?" I said with a smile. "Only, I have a very special night planned." Okay, I wasn't feeling like a seductress but I wouldn't let him know that.

He leaned in and kissed me. I knew where this was going. It was going through the door, up the stairs and into my bed. He was mine for tonight. He would love the underwear. He would love the killer heels that I had in store. He would love the bikini wax. He'd love it all. Beverley had promised me that he'd love everything and now I was finally beginning to trust her. My desire for him was off the scale. I grabbed his hand and led him to the door. "I have to go. I just wanted to make sure you got back safely." He let go of my hands. "I've been feeling a bit dicky since the fish," he said.

What? Had I heard right. Why hadn't he mentioned this before? He'd let me think all along he was coming back with me. Was I that out of practice at reading signals? Stupid desperate woman Annie, I thought. Stupid, stupid, stupid. My desire dropped to that of an ice cube, in the Arctic, on the day of a winter blizzard, during an ice age. Maybe this trip was a bad idea or maybe he was genuinely feeling ill. "Is it me?"

He kissed me gently before he began to walk away. "No, it's my bad stomach. Come on a boat trip with me tomorrow. I've reserved two places in the hope that you would. Be at the marina at nine. I'll be looking out for you."

He did like me. Maybe it was just the fish. What if I get a dicky belly? I ate some of the fish. Only time will tell I suppose. The eye of evil flashed through my mind, well it wasn't really evil but the eye in the fish looked evil to me. Maybe the fish was about to get its revenge.

"I'll be there," I called back. He blew me a kiss, turned and walked at a fast pace. I wondered where he was staying. I realised we'd spoke most of the evening but I still knew very little about him. I have no idea where he works or what he even does for a living. I know he has a son and an ex-wife but that's about it. He worked in Newcastle but doesn't any more. How can I still know so little? Jason remains a mystery for now, one I'm determined to crack very soon.

I looked at my watch. Ten-thirty and I was in for the night. I passed the concierge or should I say the chap watching rubbish on the television. He didn't acknowledge me. This place was a prize dump.

Boats, bikinis and fishy goings on

Bikini looking good – check. Maxi dress feeling good – check. Hair tied up in loose bun – check. Factor thirty – check. Sun hat – I'd hate to get burned. Kindle – I don't think I need it. I think I should be making an effort to get to know Jason a little better than I did last night. I placed my kindle on the dressing table. Thankfully, I'd made it through the night without puking which means the little bit of fish I ate was perfectly good fish. I hope Jason is well. I hope his tummy trouble was just nerves and not the fish, after all, food poisoning could render our holiday ruined. I dashed into the bathroom to check my make-up one last time. Waterproof make-up should stay on all day, right? Could it survive the sea? The cistern continued to drip. I'd complained last night but the chap just nodded. He didn't even take a note. Note to myself, be sure to leave an online review when I get home. I don't even think this place should be open to the public. I checked the time. It was eight-thirty, time to head off to the marina and seek Jason out. He'd better not stand me up.

I grabbed my bag and slammed the door as I left. I've found that slamming it forces it to catch the lock. The concierge was asleep at the desk when I passed. No doubt he'd been watching tripe on TV all night. As I left the hotel, the heat hit me. Sweat gathered around my hairline. I put my hat on and headed towards the seafront, walking past all the cafés and hotel frontages. My destination was in sight. Keep going along the promenade, past the ice-cream stall and past the statue of Ataturk. Boats were revving up, boat owners were calling tourists and offering scuba diving, pirate boat trips and fishing. I hope our boat isn't a fishing boat. Yesterday's encounter with fish was enough. I'm not sure what I think about the prospect of scuba diving either. I waited by a small trip boat. A simple wooden structure with a small upstairs.

"Annie," a man called. I turned expecting to see Jason but it was only Gavin. He left his party behind and walked over to me. "Are you on a trip today?"

"Yes. I'm just waiting here for my friend," I replied. Was Jason my friend? I think friend is a safe term at this stage in our relationship. In my fantasies, he's been far more than a friend. Does stroking my leg in a restaurant and a past fling equal more? Gavin pulled out two bottles of water from his sports bag and passed me one. I accepted it and took a swig. "Thank you."

"We're on this boat. It leaves in ten minutes. Which one are you on?"

I looked up and down. Jason was nowhere to be seen. "I'm not sure. My friend booked the boat trip and I'm meant to be meeting him here." Now I felt self-conscious. Gavin knew that my friend was a he and 'he' hadn't turned up. I began to bite the corner of my nail.

"You'll ruin your beautiful nails if you keep eating them," he said. I couldn't make out his eyes through his sunglasses. For a moment, I thought he might be looking at me a little longer than was needed to gauge my reaction to his statement. He'd noticed my nails. I looked away. "Pink, it suits you." How could he tell they were pink with his sunglasses on? He must've seen them on the plane.

"Dad. We need to get on the boat," Andy called. The rest of his party shouted and laughed as they stepped into the cabin and filtered to the top deck. A couple of young women also got on the boat.

"Join us if you want," Gavin said. I gazed up at him. If Jason didn't turn up in the next couple of minutes, I would take him up on that offer. Jason was a strange one. Maybe my original instinct was right and his dodgy tummy had been an excuse to ditch me last night. By going on a boat trip with Andy's Stag Do, I could at least salvage the day.

"I'm so sorry I'm late," Jason said as he approached me from behind, panting and holding a fishing rod. "You found the boat." Please let it not be a fishing boat, I thought as I gazed around at the line of boats before me.

Gavin left us alone and joined his son on the boat. "Catch you later," he called as he left.

Jason glanced at Gavin then passed our tickets to the skipper. We walked along the plank and into the same cabin as Andy's Stag Do. We were on the same boat as Andy's stag party. I can't think of anything less romantic at this point. I suppose that Gavin had now guessed that the red tickler condoms he'd recommended in the airport had a purpose and that purpose was Jason. While I'm thinking about it, why does Jason have a fishing rod?

Jason led me to the top deck and threw the rod under his sun lounger. Maybe he'd hoped to do a bit of fishing while we were on board. I placed my towel on a sun-bed and looked away. I'd have to remove my dress at some point and expose my body. It's hilarious isn't it? Only a few hours ago, I was ready to whip everything off and embark on a passionate night with him but now, in the light of day, I felt reluctant to remove my dress when I had a bikini on. Andy's friend thundered up the stairs and the boat began to chug in the calm Aegean Sea. A mass of twenty somethings filled the decks. The lad who'd been wearing the wacky plastic glasses on a previous occasion was responding to someone calling him Connor. Wacky glasses was called Conner. I suppose I'd get to know them better over the course of the day.

"Are you joining me for a sunbathe?" Jason called. He'd already taken his tee-shirt off. He was tanned and wore a pair of green and yellow swimming shorts. I looked at my arms. I'd caught a little sun but mostly I'd turned pink and freckly. It would take several days for my skin to bronze. The pin-up bikini had been my favourite purchase. I felt that the high waist disguised my lumpy belly and the generous cups had accentuated my womanly curves. Navy and white with red trimmings. Beverley had said they were my colours. Why wasn't I feeling very womanly? I struggled to pull my dress over my head. My bun got caught in the straps and my sweaty mound of hair flopped into my eyes. "Want a hand?"

He got off his sun lounger and untangled my straps, then he lifted my dress over my head. I turned and stood in front of him, waiting for a compliment. Surely he would like the bikini. Beverley had promised me he would love the bikini. I looked him up and down. He moved in closer. I tilted my head and closed my eyes, waiting for his kiss. "I'll just get us a beer," he shouted. How had he got from right beside me to the top of the steps in the moment it took me to close my eyes and reopen them? I couldn't work him out. My mystery man was becoming more mysterious by the second. I watched as we left the marina. People were everywhere now, families playing on the promenade, children running around and others sitting in the café by the taxi area. A little boy was standing on the pavement waving at the boat. I smiled and waved back. I guess he was maybe five or six years old. His mother caught up with him and grabbed his hand, pulling him into the shade. I knew how she felt. It was hard work looking after little ones. I wondered how my little ones were getting on.

I screamed and jumped forward. "He made me do it," shouted Connor as he looked back at one of the other lads. The cheeky sod was standing there holding the cold beer he'd just pressed against my back.

"It wasn't me I swear," the other lad shouted as he laughed uncontrollably.

"I'm sorry Annie, I thought you'd think it was funny," Connor said. "It's your beer anyway."

I realised I'd been giving him my stern classroom look, the one I saved for when the children in my class had been exceptionally trying. I broke into laughter. It had been cool and nice. Forget the fact that I nearly jumped overboard to escape the cold attack. "Thanks for the beer," I said as I took it off him.

"Don't thank me. Your boyfriend asked me to give it to you," he replied.

My boyfriend? Oh, he means Jason. Where was Jason? I took the beer and smiled. I wrapped my sarong around my waist and climbed down the steps to find Jason drinking with the rest of the stag party. "Have you come to join us?" he asked.

"I thought you were just going to get a drink."

"I was but I got held up with these maniacs," Jason said as he swigged his beer and jeered with the group. It was at this point I was beginning to think he didn't like me much. Why would he want to bring me on a boat trip then ignore me to drink with a stag party he wasn't part of? One of the young women joined them and sat next to Jason. They all looked like they were having stacks of fun without me. I looked out to sea and noticed that we were too far away to go back. If I could've got off at that point I would have, but I'm bad at swimming, really bad, so I suppose I'm stuck. I walked to the front of the boat alone and gazed out at the sea. I wished I'd brought my kindle. Never mind, maybe I should just catch some sun. I headed back to my sun-bed, plastered on my own sun cream and closed my eyes.

*****

I prised my eyes open. The sun almost blinded me. Why was I covered up? I'd been lying on my back to try and tan my front. I checked my phone. Had we really been on the boat two hours? I pulled the sarong off my chest.

"Hope you don't mind, my dad covered you up, said something about you getting burned," Andy said.

"I must thank him in a bit," I said with a smile. I heard laughing and jeering coming from the deck below. Amongst the voices, Jason's boomed out. Anyone would think it was his party. He had some making up to do if this relationship was going any further. I heard plates and pans being scraped along a surface. The savoury kofta aroma reached my nostrils. I was officially starving. I'd skipped breakfast so that I wouldn't bloat up in my bikini. As for making that level of effort now, I'd given up. I was going to eat until I could eat no more. I stumbled off the sun lounger, put my sunglasses on and made my way down.

"I've saved you a seat for lunch," Jason called. I walked over to him and shuffled along the bench to sit beside him. Gavin was sitting at the other end of the boat. I would remember to thank him later. I watched Jason through my sunglasses. Was he watching the two younger women on the boat? I'm sure he was.

"It was lovely of you to bring me out for the day but I may as well have come on my own," I said, hoping that my disappointment came through loud and clear.

"I'm so sorry. I got talking to some of the lads and you know how it is. I thought you'd enjoy a little sunbathe on your own."

"I'd have preferred a little sunbathe with you." I looked away willing the tear in the corner of my eye to go away. I will not have him seeing me upset.

He placed his sweaty hand on my knee. "I'm so sorry. Can we start again? We still have a couple of stops on the boat. We can still have fun." I gave him my hand and forced a smile. I was being unreasonable. He'd just been making friends with the rest of the passengers. I needed to lighten up and join in. A plate of chicken, salad and koftas got placed on the table. The skipper then left and went below the cabin to join the rest of his crew for lunch.

I tucked in, enjoying the lovely food. Maybe I was just hungry and it was making me grouchy. He kissed me on the forehead and put his arm around my shoulder. "Have you seen the fish?" he asked. I looked at the sea. Some of the party had thrown a few chunks of bread into the sea and the fish were coming up to eat it.

I reached out and put my arm around him. "I'm sorry too. I was being silly," I said. I wasn't giving up on my dream at the first hurdle. The boat started up.

*****

"Next stop, swimming in the cove," the skipper shouted. Swimming, I'm not good at swimming. I can manage a doggy paddle but I really like my feet to touch the ground.

I heard the anchor being released. Jason pulled me to the side of the boat. "Wow, the sea looks amazing. We have to go in," he said as he pulled my sarong off and dropped it on the chair.

"I can't swim that well," I said, hoping he'd let me off. Three lads cannonballed from the top deck into the sea below. I felt the cool flecks of water splash my face as they landed.

"Have this," Gavin said as he reached over my shoulder and passed me an orange rubber ring. I blushed and took it off him. He nudged past me and dived into the sea. Jason followed him, leaving me and the two young women behind. I cringed as I stepped into the water with the rubber ring around my waist. All thoughts of looking sexy and elegant had long passed. I looked silly in a rubber ring. I removed the rubber ring and threw it back on deck. I could swim a little. I'd stay close to the ladders and doggy paddle my way around.

I lowered my body into the water, gasping as I adjusted to the cool temperature. I could do this. I closed my eyes and began to flap my hands in front of me. Jason came back up and splashed water in my face. I'd lost my way; which way was I going? I reached out to grab the ladders but they'd gone. My head bobbed under the water. I bobbed back up and coughed. I still couldn't see. My eyes were glazed over and the sun was blinding me. I tried to reach for the ladders again. I heard people laughing and splashing. "Help me," I shouted as I grabbed Jason's shoulders.

"It's okay. Hold onto me," he said as he grabbed my other hand and placed it on his shoulder. Slowly, my vision returned to normal. Jason swam, taking me with him. I never imagined for one moment that I'd swim in the sea but I had. Beverley would be impressed. Did my minuscule effort count as actual swimming? It would when I told Beverley.

We were called back onto the boat for our last stop at a little village called Turunç. Everyone else clambered back onto the boat. Jason helped me to the ladder and gave me a push up. As I hauled my body out of the water my bikini top filled with water and pulled downwards from my breasts, exposing both of them in full to the stag party. They jeered and laughed. Were they laughing at me or were they just merry? I couldn't tell. I pulled at my bikini top and shoved my boobs back in the cups. "That deserves a beer," Gavin said as he passed me a bottle of Efes. They had jeered at me. Red wine lady with her red tickler condoms was now a flasher. I needed to head back to my sun lounger to hide for a while.

*****

The walk around the village was almost coming to an end and that would be the end of our day. We'd had coffee and cake at one of the cafés and ambled around the streets looking in the windows of gift shops. He'd even bought me a fridge magnet of Marmaris Castle so that we'd always remember this moment. I wondered how the evening was going to pan out. Maybe Jason would come back to mine and have a shower or maybe something else. The morning had been a bit strange but he'd since made up for it. He'd helped me in the sea, rubbed lotion on my back and even gave me a foot massage. "What's happening tonight?" I asked.

"What do you want to happen tonight?" he replied.

I smiled and started playing with my frizzy hair. "Well, maybe you could come and meet me at my apartment and we could take it from there."

He leaned over and kissed me. "That sounds like a good idea. I could come over about nine"

"Nine. You can come back with me now and we can shower together," I replied. I felt fluttery as he continued to kiss me, trembling for more. I wanted to stay here forever with Jason's arms wrapped around me. I looked over his shoulder at the boats and froze.

"Jason?"

"Yes." He stroked my hair and looked into my eyes.

"Our boat has left. Maybe we could stay here for the night. Check into a hotel, any hotel, like we did ten years ago. What do you say?"

He let go of me and ran towards the boats. "We need a taxi now."

"Are you coming back to mine then?"

"I need to get back. I have to get showered and we'll meet tonight. Damn. My fishing rod is still on the boat," he yelled as he ran into the streets trying to find a taxi.

After a silent journey back, the taxi reached my apartment. Jason held the door open for me. I suppose he needed to drop me off and go back to rescue his stupid fishing rod. "Can you grab my towel too when you get your rod?" I asked. He nodded, kissed me and got back into the taxi. I wasn't too worried. The only thing I'd left on the boat was my towel.

"I'll see you here at nine," he said as the taxi pulled off. The concierge was gone. It was just me, alone with my flip-flop steps echoing around a soulless building.

It has been a good day and a bad day. I have no idea what to make of it. Maybe I'd expected too much. Ten years had passed. Maybe the spark just wasn't as strong as back then. He still keeps giving me signals though. Why does he keep kissing me? Why does he still keep arranging things for us to do? He must like me but there is something strange about him. He never did do any fishing either. There's definitely something fishy going on.

He will love the shoes!

I don't know how I'd managed to doze off but I had. I'd awoken on my balcony to the sound of a car horn. I'd had an hour to get ready before Jason was picking me up. In that hour I'd managed to wedge my behind into the little black number that Beverley had chosen. I'd straightened my hair, applied my make-up and I was now toying with wearing the killer heels. I still hadn't forgiven them for my fall down the stairs.

To wear or not to wear? That is the question. What would Shakespeare do if he was writing a farce called, Annie's Trip? I think he'd make her wear the shoes. He'd ensure that she suffered total humiliation but all would be right in the end as long as Annie's Trip wasn't a tragedy. I don't want this evening to end in a bloodbath. I'd already suffered the humiliation bit when I'd fallen down the stairs in front of Mallory. Maybe I've had my fair share and my story was turning a corner. I smiled and grabbed the killer heels. If he doesn't melt when he sees the killer heels then I have no chance whatsoever of my happy ever after. How had I become so fixated on happy ever after? This is only a holiday meet up with a fling of days gone by, but don't we all really want to meet the one? I'd kidded myself for a long time, thinking my job and the girls were enough but they weren't. There we go. I'm a woman and I'm declaring that I'm not satisfied with life. I want a companion, I want a lover, I want a confidante, and I want a man. Jason could be all those.

Another one of those pesky beetle like insects scurried across the floor as I gazed at myself in the mirror. I picked up my phone to check the time. It was eight-fifty. Ten minutes until pick up time. That's a whole ten minutes to make myself look the best I can. A little more mascara, a little more red lipstick. Blusher, I need more rouge. I leaned back to examine my look. Was it a little too Rocky Horror? I grabbed a wipe and removed the lipstick. Beverley was totally wrong about the lipstick. It's just not me. It's not Annie now and it wasn't Annie of ten years ago. The black dress looks good though. I stood and turned in front of the mirror. I was curvy but the dress was so right for the curves. Black mini dress, leopard print killer heels, I was ready to make my mark on Marmaris.

I grabbed the handrail and took careful steps until I reached reception. "Have a good night Miss," the concierge said without taking his eyes of the TV screen. The reception clock told me that it was five past nine. Jason deserved to be kept waiting after this morning so I didn't feel too guilty. Maybe now he'd know how it felt.

As I step out of reception and onto the path outside, I know I can't look like a new born horse when I walk. I have to walk with some level of confidence.

I took a deep breath, opened the door and stepped it out like I was on a catwalk, all the way to the road. I'd made it without tripping. I wanted to jump up and down and do a victory dance. Where was Jason? Was he late again? I stared up and down the road, he was nowhere to be seen. Every time a taxi passed, my heart skipped a beat in the hope that it was him coming to get me. I watched as the man sitting outside the bag shop opposite sipped his tea.

Ten minutes passed, twenty minutes passed. My feet were pinching. As I crouched to sit on the curb, I'm sure my dress rode up and exposed my pants. The man on the opposite side of the road laughed as he entered his shop. Another fifteen minutes passed. I watched the cars and buses go up and down. It was me, alone in the darkness, waiting for someone who would never arrive. My instincts were right. Jason had never had an upset stomach; Jason hadn't been attentive. He'd met me for a quickie at the castle and when I wouldn't go back with him right there and then, he'd felt me not worth too much of an effort. I still couldn't work out why he'd not spoken to me in the morning on the boat trip. Why had he stayed below deck and left me alone? Why would he go to all the trouble of meeting again today when he could've just said last night that it wasn't working for him? I could've just got on with enjoying my holiday. I hadn't felt this emotionally drained since my teen years. At forty-five, you think I'd have all this worked out but really, the older I get, I think people become more complicated. Should finding love be this complicated? "Can I get you a taxi Miss?" I flinched and looked up. The concierge spoke while looking at me for the first time since I'd checked in. Great, even he could see me for the sad case that I was.

I nodded. "Thank you, that's very kind of you." He walked into the road and flagged a passing taxi. I had no idea where I wanted to go. Concierge man went back into the hotel. The small flicker of charm within him had come and gone before I could stand. "To the marina," I said. The driver turned his music up and drove.

I have no plan, I have no aim, and I have no reasons. It's just me in a taxi heading to the marina. I paid and got out, passed the café on the corner by the tourist office and headed inwards. Maybe I would check out Bar Street myself. "Join us for a drink," a lad shouted as he gyrated to the music that was booming out of the first bar I passed. I certainly was easy picking. One word from him and I was in his bar. There's nothing like being stood up to make you susceptible to charm, after all, my self-esteem had taken a battering. I ordered two vodka and cokes, yes two. Don't judge me too harshly for drinking in twos but I need them. I need to be alone, surrounded by loud music and flashing lights, to wallow in my rejection. I caught a glance of my reflection. Who was I kidding? I can see why he didn't come. Beverley had made me feel good about myself, dressed me up like a doll and told me how wonderful I looked. I stared at my lumpy hips that had expanded the material on the dress. In fact, it wasn't just my hips, it was my stomach and my arms. I'm trying to be realistic here, I can't deny I have bingo wings and I'm sleeveless. What the hell was I thinking? I kicked the shoes to the floor and smiled, at least I hadn't fallen over. Things could always be worse. I chugged the one drink back and pushed the empty aside.

The dance floor got busier and busier by the minute as people began to spill in. It was a shame that most of the people were a lot younger than me. I spotted Wacky Glasses, I mean Connor, dancing with one of the young women from the boat trip. They gyrated together. He had his tongue down her throat as he grabbed her tiny behind and pulled her into his groin. I have developed an obsession with tiny behinds. I thought of Mallory and my ex-husband. I bet he loves her little firm behind. I need a personal trainer. When I get home, I'm going to the gym, I'm not eating chips and chocolate. Everything will be home cooked. I need to get myself back in the race for love.

"Wow and more wow," Gavin shouted over the music. I hadn't seen him come in but then again my eyes had been fixed on all the young lovelies while I was quietly envying their firm young figures and berating myself for not being perfect. "You look stunning Annie."

I looked away and smiled. What do I say? If I say thank you, I'm accepting that I am stunning. If I say don't be silly, I'm essentially being rude. I went to speak but I couldn't say a word. I looked away again and took a swig of my drink.

"Can I get you another?" he asked.

The vodka had certainly warmed me up. "Surprise me." Stuff Jason. If he couldn't be bothered to meet me, I was going to have a hell-of-a night out, and Gavin seemed a nice guy. I could enjoy a dance and a laugh with Gavin and spend tomorrow having a real think about where my life was going. Gavin smiled and went to the bar. I watched as a barman prepared a fruity looking thing in a tall glass with a sparkler sticking out of the top. Cocktail time had arrived.

"Sex on the beach, a classic," Gavin said as he helped me get my shoes back on, and led me away from the speaker to the buildings frontage. "I can hear better over here," he shouted.

"Thank you, for the drink." I sipped and grimaced. Bloody hell it was strong but just what I needed. I wanted to loosen up and have a good night.

"What brings you here alone?"

I looked down and shook my head. Do I tell my new friend Gavin all about my escapade? Do I tell him that I've been stood up? I looked out of the window. "It's complicated," I replied.

"I thought that when I saw him eating with his family about an hour ago by the marina. You're better than that Annie, you deserve more," he said as he placed a friendly hand on my shoulder. I felt a tear welling in my eye. I should've known. The signs were hitting me in the face at every turn. He'd had to rush away one too many times. I thought back to the little boy waving to me on the boat. Was he waving at Jason? Was Jason his daddy? Had he told them he was going on a fishing trip for the day to put them off joining him? I've been so stupid. I felt tears falling down my face. I'm not sure if I was crying because of Jason or because of all the years I'd wasted thinking about him.

"I didn't know," I said as I sobbed. That's when it all came out. "We made a pact ten years ago to meet at Marmaris Castle. I couldn't believe it when he actually turned up but it hadn't been right. Something had been missing this time. He's not single, that's what was missing. I can't believe I fell for it. I'm so stupid. I knew it felt wrong." I said as I sobbed in my drink. Gavin removed the drink from my hand and placed it on the table. He reached over and pulled me into his chest.

"You're not stupid My Love. It's his loss," Gavin said as he stroked my hair. I don't believe him though. I am stupid. I've been a complete and utter idiot. He's humiliated me and he's humiliated his wife. What were we ever going to amount to? A big fat nothing.

I realised I was still nestled in Gavin's chest. I pulled away and looked at him. I'd smudged mascara all over his white shirt. Damn it, the stupid mascara was meant to be waterproof. Why was everything going wrong? "I'm so sorry about your shirt," I said.

"Don't worry about it. I've got another one." He handed me my drink.

"Are you alright," Andy slurred as he staggered over to his father.

"Yes, fine Son. Just go back to your dancing and drinking." Andy pointed and grinned before joining his friends back on the dance floor.

"This really isn't my idea of fun. I think Andy's managing alright on his own. He insisted that I come on his stag do which was good of him but the pace is killing me. Shall we go outside and get some air?"

I nodded and smiled. Stuff Jason, stuff it all. I was going to salvage this holiday and enjoy chatting to Gavin.

An hour passed and I felt a little giddy. Being reckless with cocktails when I have the constitution of a flea isn't the best move. At least I didn't feel sick. There's no way on earth I could drink anymore though. One more and I think I would be sick. I couldn't let Gavin see me vomiting for a second time within a week. "Can we walk the drink off?" I asked.

"Yes, sounds good, where do you want to go?"

"Up the steps. Past the castle and by the boats," I replied. I didn't worry for a minute about bumping into Jason. If he'd been there with his wife and child, he'd be long gone. It was late.

"Great," he offered me a hand up.

I tottered along the cobbled pavement. It was no good, if I continued to walk in these shoes, I was going to topple. I took them off and carried them.

"I love the shoes by the way Annie. They're some seriously sassy shoes," Gavin said with a cheeky smile. At least someone appreciated the shoes.

I hadn't taken too much notice of his features but he had quite large brown eyes. His fine hair was quite light and wispy. I wanted to touch it, feel how soft it was. I'd been so blind. Chasing Jason had been an idiotic move. I didn't even know him anymore. There was nothing there but my desire to reconnect with womanhood. I had found the fantasy of him far more attractive that the real him. The real Jason had been a bit of an arsehole, not just an arsehole but an arsehole already in a relationship. No wonder he'd been so cagy about telling me where he was staying and where he was from. Under no uncertain terms did he ever want me crossing his cosy little home life. I giggled and reached out, stroking Gavin's hair as we climbed the steps to the castle. I just couldn't resist. I stumbled as we reached the top. "You're going to cut your feet Madam," he said as he picked me up and carried me past the castle. I giggled as he stumbled in the dark, banging against the castle wall as we made our way over the hill.

I howled with laughter as we came out by the marina. Gavin tripped, dropping me on the pavement and then falling on me. A sharp pain surged through my coccyx but I couldn't stop laughing. "You dropped me."

"I dropped myself," he said, trying to control his laughter. Gavin stopped laughing and gazed into my eyes. Both of us were sprawled out in the middle of the pavement. Other revellers either stepped over us or walked around. I saw his smile begin to emerge and I burst into laughter again, setting him off too. I didn't care that people were looking, I didn't care that people were stepping over me, I didn't care that I was probably showing a bit of pantie and I certainly didn't care what any of them thought. He stumbled to a standing position and held his hand out. I grabbed it and he pulled me up. I linked my arm through his and we carried on walking. I turned to the side and looked at him again.

The giggle fit continued. I had to look away otherwise I'd never stop laughing. As I turned my head, I spotted Jason. He had his arm around a woman while looking out at the boats. A little boy, the one who was waving at me from the marina, was curled up asleep in his lap. Jason looked up and his eyes stared into mine. His wife looked up and saw me staring back. For a moment, I think all three of us had felt uneasy. Gavin scooped me up again carried me past the statue of the children, where he placed me down on the wall. We sat together giggling and watching the boats.

"I know this sounds odd but I really fancy an ice-cream," Gavin said as he stared at the boats.

"Me too." There's nothing more I wanted in the world right there and then than an ice-cream, preferably a chocolate one.

Breakfast and the man in my bed

I hadn't slept in for this long in ages. It was almost
eleven and I was still lying in bed. My head thumped a
little, probably the cocktail and vodkas. I thought back
to the night before. In many ways, it had been one of the
worst nights I'd endured in recent memory but it had
also been one of the best. I hadn't laughed so much in
years. I went to sit up and flinched. My back was
killing. I smiled as I remembered being flung to the
floor in front of loads of people at the marina. It was
worth the pain to laugh so much. I dragged my aching
body out of bed and headed to the bathroom. Smiling, I
thought back to the night before. It had been lovely
eating ice-cream at the marina. Gavin had dropped me
back in a taxi about two in the morning. We spoke for

ages and I never realised we had so much in common. We were both divorced, we both loved ice-cream, especially chocolate flavour, we were both in our forties and we were both parents. He only lived a few miles away from me and we'd agreed to meet for a drink when we got home. I glared at my hideous reflection. Why hadn't I cleaned my make-up off my face before I went to bed? I grabbed a wipe and got rid of the smeared eye liner and mascara. I remember leaving a nasty dark smudge on Gavin's crisp shirt the night before. I hope he manages to remove the stain. I brushed my teeth, trying to remove the taste of vodka and souring chocolate ice-cream from my mouth. A quick shower and I'd feel like my old self again.

The room phone rang. At least something worked. I spat the toothpaste out and ran to answer. "I have a man in reception for you. He is coming up," the charming concierge man said before placing the handset down. No hello or goodbye, just a matter of fact statement before replacing the handset. I didn't want to see Jason. Wasn't it against hotel rules to give room numbers out and let anyone in?

I stared at my reflection in the mirror. Bare faced, tired looking old woman with baggy eyes and frizzy hair. Did I care? No, I couldn't give a stuff. Jason can go and do one as far as I'm concerned. I grabbed one of my beach dresses and popped it over my head. There's no way I'd dream of answering in my bra and pants. He's already seen enough. I've laid myself bare emotionally and physically, okay not quite physically but the intention had been there.

There was a knock at the door. I took a deep breath. You can do this Annie. Just open the door and tell him where to go. I held my hand out, ready to wrestle the door open. "I don't know why the hell you thought it might be a good idea to come here after what happened. I saw you. Is she your wife? Wait, don't answer. I don't give a stuff. Just go away and don't come anywhere near me again," I yelled. My hands were shaking. I let go of the stubborn door and held my head in my hands.

"Annie."

"Gavin?"

"Sorry for coming to your hotel. I was err just popping by and thought after things went so well last night, I'd bring you some breakfast. I'd have called first but I didn't have your number. I'd never forget Bates Motel though," he replied with a laugh.

My heart began to flutter. Oh my, I was in a state, but then again I was in a state when he'd seen me the night before. "Lift and push when I say go," I said.

I pulled, he pushed. Between us, we opened the door. "How on earth are you managing like this?" he asked as he entered.

"Great difficulty." He placed a plastic container on my crumpled bedcover. I darted in front of him and turned over my mascara stained pillow.

"You didn't have to do this," I said as I kneeled in front of the bed and opened the container.

"I know. I wanted to." Gavin paused. He looked around the room and scrunched his nose in an almost cute way. I could tell he wasn't impressed with the white washed décor and the chipped furniture. His gaze came back to me. "I enjoyed last night and was wondering if you wanted to do something with me today. The lads have gone on a jeep safari and I didn't really fancy being blasted with a water cannon all day so I thought I'd just have a beach day and well I wondered, I was just thinking-" He was waffling. Was he nervous? I could tell he was nervous.

"I'd love to do something."

"Great. I hope you like Turkish breakfast."

"I love Turkish breakfast." I opened the takeaway containers and found several little pots containing cheese, meat, bread and preserves. I grabbed a couple of plates and forks from my kitchenette. We tucked in, enjoying the bread and honey. The salty olives were scrummy and I absolutely adored the rose jam. "This is delicious, thank you so much."

"You're welcome. So what are we doing today?" I licked the last of the jam off my fingers and stood in my creased dress.

He started to clear the rubbish away. "I brought my beach stuff. Fancy grabbing a sun lounger, having a few drinks and taking a relaxing dip in the sea? I bought you an inflatable rubber ring, it's in my bag," he said as he winked and laughed.

I picked up the last of the rubbish from my bed and slapped him playfully on the arm as I passed. "Piss taker."

"I'm only joking," he said as he stood.

The room then seemed small. All it contained was my bed, a small amount of furniture, this thing that the brochure described as a kitchenette and the door to the balcony but there still wasn't enough room to pass each other without touching. I smiled as I brushed past him to throw away the last of the rubbish. Did he like me? I mean, I'm standing here wearing a hideously creased dress and no make-up, and to top it all off I haven't showered yet, I probably stink to high heaven. "Why don't you make yourself at home while I have a quick shower and turn myself into a human again," I said as I threw him the remote and went into the bathroom.

Minutes later I was out of the shower and blow drying my hair straight while wearing only a towel. Why did I feel so relaxed in front of Gavin? He watched a foreign music channel as he lay on my bed with his ankles crossed. I grabbed my bikini and a fresh beach dress, then I headed back into the bathroom. There's a man lying on my bed, waiting for me to get ready so that we can go out and waste the day away together. I smiled at myself in the mirror as I pulled on my bikini. I wasn't perfect but I was me. Gavin was happy to spend the day with me, lumps, bumps and all. We'd had so many laughs the night before. I hoped there were more to come today.

I kept thinking I should try and contact Beverley and tell her what's happening but she'd never believe me. I think it's best if I wait and see what's happening myself. Only a day ago, I was imagining a whole new life with another man but he'd not been who I thought he was and he hadn't really lived up to my fantasies, and he was a rat. I suppose I could say I'm scared of just diving in without doing a risk assessment. I think that's why I won't call Beverley. She'd tell me to get straight in there, while wearing the shoes and nothing else, and I'd probably listen. Just this once though, I'm right. I know myself and I need to think this one through, for today at least. I'll see what the day brings and take it from there. He is cute though. I did enjoy stroking his hair. I'm sure if I made a play to entice him now, I'd enjoy it very much but now wasn't the right time. I'd been so wrong about things this week that I doubted my ability to read people anymore. I wanted to remain friends with Gavin when we got home to Birmingham. I wanted to see him again. His son was lovely and his son's friends had made me feel welcome on the plane and at Bar Street. Gavin had looked out for me on the plane and the boat. I forgot to thank him for saving me from sunburn.

I left the bathroom, hair intact, bikini on, fresh beach dress covering my bikini. I grabbed a towel and stuffed it in my beach bag. I turned and noticed that Gavin was sleeping. What do I do? Do I wake him or do I leave him? I crept towards the balcony and slid the patio door open. "Annie. I'm so sorry. The guys don't let me get much sleep. I'm sharing with Connor and

Will. Connor came back last night with this girl he's been transfixed with since the day we arrived. I slept for four hours on a sun lounger by the pool." He was such a good person, giving up his room to help young love.

"Maybe you can catch up on your sleep at the beach then. Ready?"

He stretched as he got off my bed.

"Oh and thank you for covering me up the other day on the sun lounger. I look hideous with sunburn."

"It was nothing." We grabbed our bags and left. The dodgy door had let us out on our first attempt. Things were looking up.

Halva, weeds and the three legged bed

We'd been on the beach for four hours. I'd shown him the photo I kept in my purse of Emily and Shelly. He said that they looked just like me and they were really cute. Gavin had even tried to teach me to do breaststroke. I managed to do four strokes in a row without sinking. We'd also agreed that I'd meet him at our local baths in Birmingham once a week when we arrived home. He said he was making it his mission to teach me to swim properly. I can't tell you how much fun I'm having. Jason? Who's Jason? That man, thingy, him. I lay there watching the calm sea as it lapped gently on the sand around my feet. Gavin had nodded off a few minutes ago. I suppose a bad sleep, coupled with a beer in the sun, was just enough to send him into a deep slumber. I watched as he breathed open-mouthed without a care in the world, totally trusting me to keep watch. I noticed the sun touching his left arm. It was time for me to repay him and cover him up so that he didn't burn. I grabbed a hand towel from my bag, crept beside him and arranged it over the sun patch. His eyes were surrounded with slight lines, and a little bit of stubble was breaking through his chin. I held my hand out over his head, so wanting to stroke his hair again. He hadn't said anything the other night after I stroked his hair. I have no idea what he thought of that strange little gesture. His broad shoulders were completely relaxed. I wondered what it would feel like to embrace him. He'd picked me up the other night by the castle, so I had a bit of idea how it would feel. He'd also dropped me. I laughed to myself as I recalled that moment. Maybe I should stroke his hair, just a little. Just a quick touch.

"Annie. I've been looking for you all over," Jason said as he approached me from behind. I went to turn and whacked Gavin on the head as I swung my arm around.

"What?" Gavin yelled as he rubbed his eyes. Great, I'd not only disturbed Gavin, I had to deal with Jason. I'd hoped never to see him again. Why had he come looking for me?

"I have nothing to say to you," I said.

Jason removed his sunglasses and his gaze flitted between Gavin and me. Gavin put his sunglasses on and stared at Jason. He then stretched and grabbed his wallet. "I'm going to grab a couple of drinks. If you need me just yell," he said, glaring at Jason as he walked off.

"It didn't take you long did it?" Jason said.

"Like you can talk Mr Family Man. Thought it would be funny to come and meet me while hiding Wifey out the way?"

"It's not like that. I made a promise to you all those years ago and I didn't want to let you down."

"You didn't want to let me down. The kindest thing you could've done was not turn up and let me forget you. Instead, you turn up and lie to me. Do you know what you've put me through?" I shouted. He turned away. "I binned your stupid fridge magnet by the way. Marmaris bloody Castle."

He crouched down under my sunshade. "I've said I'm sorry. I don't know how to put this right. I thought we might just be able to have a bit of holiday fun."

"We or you. None of it has been fun for me." A couple on the sun loungers next to me looked up. "Sorry," I said, knowing that I'd disturbed them.

"I wanted to apologise anyway. I really am sorry. I brought you these," he said as he pulled out a box of halva and a handful of weeds.

"Why have you brought me a pile of weeds?"

"They weren't weeds when I picked them." He began pacing up and down beside my sun lounger. "They're flowers. It's hot, they need some water."

"Dr Frankenstein couldn't resuscitate these," I replied.

He dropped the dead flowers on the end of my sun lounger. "I don't know what else to say."

"Sometimes it's best to say nothing and leave it at that." My body tensed and people began to stare. The couple next to me packed their towels away and left the beach. Why was he doing this to me? Hadn't he let me down enough? Didn't he have a wife and child to attend to? The sleaze bag. I thought of Mallory. Had she felt my rage when she found out Phillip was married? I wondered if Jason was happy in his marriage, I hope he isn't as I find it despicable that he's treating his wife this way if he's pretending to be the loving husband. I shook my head. Phillip and I were different; we weren't in love. I don't think even Phillip could've done this to me.

"I'm going to say one more thing and then I'll leave. Ten years from now, seven in the evening. Meet me at Marmaris Castle. Our circumstances may have changed by then. Who knows? Will you do that?" he asked as he looked into my eyes. I grabbed my flip-flop and threw it at him.

"Get lost and don't come near me again." He stepped back and dropped the halva on the sand. I almost fell off the sun lounger as I leaned across and grabbed the box. I flung it so hard he jumped as it hit his arm. "We should've left our fling where it belonged, in the past. Now, go away, find your wife and work on being a good husband." Why was he standing there staring at me? "Leave me alone."

"Annie-"

"Don't Annie me, just go away. How many times do I have to tell you?" I said as I turned away. I heard footsteps approaching. Gavin walked towards me with a couple of glasses of lemonade.

"You heard her," Gavin said as he placed the drinks down on the table. "Leave her alone."

"Or else what?"

Gavin grabbed the pile of weeds off my sun lounger, walked over to Jason and slammed them into his chest. "Just go now." The weeds fell to the floor in a small pile. The sea breeze blew a couple of the lighter ones across the sand.

Jason took a few deep breaths, stared at Gavin then turned and marched along the beach until he was out of sight. "I'm so sorry," I said. I started packing my things away. Would Gavin now realise that I was more trouble than I was worth? "I best get going. Have a shower and whatever."

"Why are you going?"

"Why would you want me stay? You know why I came to Marmaris."

"I know why you came. You came here to find yourself, to feel like a woman again, to have fun and enjoy a holiday. Here's the big reveal, you can still do all those things."

I dropped my bag and scraped my hair back with my hands. A tear meandered down my cheek. Gavin stepped closer and placed his arms around me. "Come on Annie. There's so much to enjoy. Get in that sea, we're going to start learning backstroke," he said as he pulled away and dragged me into the water. I sobbed as I laughed. He dragged me further into the sea until we were waist height. I looked at the sun shining through his hair. I wish he wasn't wearing sunglasses; I can't read his expression. Do I need to read it? Or do I just think about how I feel and go with it? Beverley, what do I do? I know you're not going to answer because you're not here in my head, but that doesn't stop me asking the question. He led me further into the sea, walking backwards while holding both of my hands.

"Wait," I whispered.

"What is it? Scared?"

I wasn't scared. I leaned in before I could change my mind and allowed my lips to brush his. Please respond, I thought. Please kiss me back. I leaned out. What had I done? He grabbed me and kissed me so hard, in a way that no one had ever kissed me before. His lips locked against mine. My whole body felt weightless and it wasn't just the salty sea creating that effect. His firm arms wrapped around me. I placed my arms further round his neck and ran my fingers through his hair. If I summed this moment up, I would say it was the most erotic moment of my entire life. I'm a forty-five year old woman and nothing has ever prepared me for this moment. I don't know how to react. Gavin wanting me matters too much. I'm scared I'll say something wrong. I want his hands to trail over my body but they don't. He keeps me in his grip and wanting more, but making me wait. What would Annie of ten years ago say about this? Younger Annie would be totally envious. He is what younger Annie would be prepared to wait a long time for. She's waited long enough. I need to get in there now and create my own destiny. I need to be prepared to put my desires out there for him to see and if they're not reciprocated, then so be it. No games, no hiding of feelings, just the truth. I'm now here, taking what I want from life, taking this moment for myself.

"Come back to mine. I have a pack of red ticklers that need testing," I whispered. He took off his sunglasses and looked at me.

"I had no idea you were like that Annie," he said, then he laughed.

I scooped up some water and splashed him and ran, packing up my things and then his things. He stumbled to the sun lounger and grabbed both towels. It felt so naughty luring him back to the Bates Motel. We ran, soaking wet, past the concierge who once again didn't take any notice. We fled up the stairs. I slipped on a step at one point, but I'd felt no pain as my knee caught a sharp edge. We reached the door and I grabbed, shoved and pulled but the door wouldn't budge. "Allow me," Gavin said as he shoulder slammed the door. It flew open. My hero. He lifted me up and carried me over the threshold as my feet and arms bashed into everything. He turned me around by the TV. The remote and a stack of tourist leaflets flew to the floor. Did we care? Did we hell?

He threw me onto the bed and I felt a drop as one of the legs crunched. Did we care? Not a bit. I rejoiced as his mouth covered mine. Did we even close the door? I haven't changed that much. I peered over his shoulder. The door was closed thank goodness. I groaned as his kisses left my mouth and trailed down my neck. I felt his hardness though his shorts, my desire was peaking and I not only needed him, I needed him now. I fumbled one handed with the bedside drawer as I reached from the lopsided bed. The red ticklers were coming out. Ooh yes, more please, and he gave me more and more and more. This is where I stop talking ....

Airports, delays and dodgy suitcases

I smiled my way through the long hot coach journey. I smiled all the way through the horrendous queue at check in. I smiled through the prices at Dalaman Airport, settling only for a bottle of water. I even smiled my way through the two-hour delay. Why was I smiling so much even though we were going home? Easy, every moment of that journey was another moment spent with Gavin. I couldn't care how late the flight was or when I got home. The girls weren't back for two more weeks and I knew that the taxi driver who was collecting me would be keeping an eye on arrivals. Gavin had surprised me with a burger meal while we waited. He'd even offered me a glass of wine before we took off.

After the last episode I had with wine, I decided to stick with my water instead.

*****

We were now over halfway home. Connor had swapped seats so that Gavin could sit by me. I was wearing his hoodie and happily snuggling against his arm while we flew. "Thanks for a wonderful holiday," I said as I stroked his arm. He leaned over and kissed my head.

"Soppy bastard," Andy said as he walked back from the toilet. A couple of the lads leaned over the seats and laughed.

"Don't speak too quick Andy. I know you're taken and all so you don't count but apart from Connor, your dad was the only member of the group to pull," Andy's friend said.

"Hey you lot. Show a bit of respect," Gavin yelled with a grin across his face. It was true. He had well and truly pulled me. I felt a little sorry for Connor. He really liked the girl he'd met on the boat but she'd dumped him just before we'd left to come home, stating that he was just a bit of holiday fun. At least she didn't leave him full of hope like Jason had with me. At least he could go home and start afresh.

I smiled as I closed my eyes and thought about all the good times we'd had over the past three days. We'd eaten out between bedroom sessions. My swimming was improving, I can now manage about ten strokes without sinking. My floatation technique is still non-existent. We'd walked along the beach at night, admiring the lights of the town. We'd spoken for hours, almost until daylight. Gavin had spent the rest of the holiday in my dump of an apartment as he was sick of sharing with the lads. Apparently when he went back to check on his apartment, Matt had thrown up on the floor and dumped a towel over the mess. The thought made me shudder. Gavin left with his clothes and some more of the red ticklers, which I was really thankful for. He said compared to his room, my room was a luxury haven. We'd eaten in bed, he'd bought me ice-cream from the shop next door. We'd showered together, hell, I'd even allowed him to use my toothbrush on the first morning as he'd forgotten his. Not even Phillip had ever used my toothbrush. He'd told me about the dream house in Shropshire that he'd just finished building, the one he'd designed and worked so hard on for the past six years. I hoped I'd get to see it one day. My heart fluttered as I rubbed his arm. I didn't want this holiday to end but I knew in about an hour we were getting off the plane.

"Are we still on for those swimming lessons when we get home?" I asked as I leaned over and pinched one of his crisps.

"What a question. I think I have my work cut out teaching you to swim," he replied. I needed that answer. I couldn't bear to leave him at Birmingham airport and never see him again. I've already imagined him being in my house. I've imagined his toothbrush in the holder next to mine and I've already picked out a section of my wardrobe for his clothes. Thinking too fast Annie. Calm down, I tell myself. I know I sound desperate but maybe I am. I've experienced something I've never felt before and I don't want to lose it. I helped myself to another crisp and crunched away. "We will continue with breaststroke, this Saturday," he said as he squeezed my hand. I squeezed back. I daren't tell him where my thoughts have been wandering to. I look up at him. He's now wearing his glasses. I've only seen him wearing them when he reads but he's kept them on throughout the flight. I like his glasses. He takes them off and rubs his eyes with his free hand. I stroke his hair.

"What are you doing this week, between now and next Saturday?" I asked.

"Well, that's up to you," he replied. What's up to me? Should I suggest something?

"I see. Maybe we could meet up tomorrow or Sunday and do something," I said as I took another crisp and crunched. He was playing with me, waiting for me to make the move. "Maybe you could come to mine tomorrow night and check out my bedroom. It's a really nice bedroom in an older house. Maybe you could give me your architectural opinion on the alcove up the far end. It contains my bed." I couldn't be any more direct. Wow, I've changed and I love the new me.

"You want my architectural opinion on your alcove?" he smiled. I wanted to kiss him so badly but his son was still leaning over occasionally.

"Very much so. It's a very unique alcove."

"What makes it unique?"

97

"It has a curvy elegance about it. It's not as modern as it could be and it might need a little updating but it has solid foundations. It's sturdy and not likely to break easily. I might even dress it up a bit, add a splash of colour, maybe leopard print."

"I'd love to take a look at your alcove tomorrow night." He leaned over and kissed me. I had secured a date. He knew my address, he'd taken my phone number and we'd even connected on Facebook. I'd had a look through his profile and he was who he said he was, an architect from Birmingham. His profile told me that he had one son called Andy and he loved sci-fi films. As I love a bit of sci-fi too, I can see us enjoying some cosy nights in this winter.

*****

We soon landed back in Birmingham. Luggage collection passed with ease and my taxi driver sent me a text informing me that he was on his way. We waited in the car park for our respective lifts. The lads went ahead, leaving Gavin and me alone. I had about five minutes and then we'd part, until tomorrow that was.

Their mini bus arrived first. "I'll see you tomorrow Annie. Call me later." I smiled and hugged him. I felt him grip me. The smell of my shampoo in his hair turned me on slightly. What was happening to me?

"Dad, come on. We have to get out of this car park in five minutes otherwise we'll have to pay a fortune," Andy shouted.

"Coming Son." He passed his case to Andy. "Safe journey home Annie Henderson. Maybe we could get away to Shropshire next weekend."

"I'd love that," I called as he stepped into the mini bus.

Was it all a dream? Had I not met the most amazing man ever? If he doesn't answer the phone later or he messes me about, I will cry, big time. He waved as the minibus pulled out of the car park. I smiled until I could see him no longer. Gavin wasn't going to let me down. We'd been too close. Our meeting was under the weirdest of circumstances but hey, so what, I think we're meant to be. I will allow myself to enjoy this moment. I will allow myself to hope and will push any doubts to the back of my mind.

I checked my phone. The rest of my messages had come through. I opened a text with a load of photo attachments. I flicked through the photos of Shelly and Emily in front of the Disney Castle followed by a photo of them coming down a water shoot. The last photo I opened was one of Phillip, Mallory and the girls. They looked so happy together I almost felt a twinge of envy. Mallory's big beaming smile filled the screen as she hugged the girls. "Don't be silly Annie," I whispered. I realised the girls had two families now, they had me, and they had their dad and Mallory. I needed their dad and Mallory to provide this kind of stability when they had the girls. I also had Gavin, maybe we would be making these kind of memories in the near future, who knows?

My taxi beeped. I hadn't noticed the driver pull in. I dragged my case over the curb and it landed with a thud, expelling all my dirty holiday clothes. A man, who looked to be in his sixties walked over to assist me. How had I ended up with Gavin's pants in my case? I blushed as the man handed me an empty red tickler box. Why hadn't I thrown that in the bin? The man winked as I took the box. "I'm glad you had a lovely time," he said as he re-joined the woman who'd now caught him up. Why wasn't my face burning? Annie of a week ago would have been red faced by now. She'd be struggling to explain herself. Not now though, I was a changed woman. Time to go home, shower, put the washing on and look forward to seeing Gavin tomorrow. My phone beeped again. A string of messages from Beverley all came through at once, all enquiring as to how my love life was going. Had I got some stories to tell her over coffee in the morning.

Creamy mochas and younger men

Second load in the washer – check. Chatted to the girls on FaceTime – check. Mallory looked a little sick, oh the joys of pregnancy. Called Gavin – check. I smiled as I remembered our phone call in my head. I was really going to stay with him next weekend at his dream house in Shropshire. He was also coming to mine tonight. I'd been and bought a couple of steaks. Steak and chips was going to be dish of the day. "Dessert – check. I hope he likes lemon meringue. I remember him liking lemon slices in his cocktails. Beverley waved from our usual table. I'd have to apologise for being a few minutes late. "Large mocha with whipped cream," the barista called. I grabbed my drink and headed over to Beverley.

"Well, spill all," she said as I was sitting. I opened my mouth to reply but she stopped me. "Wait, don't tell me. You have a special smile on your face. It went well." I went to talk. "Shh, let me carry on. He turned up, you had the week of a lifetime and the bikini wax paid off. Now you can talk."

At last I could get a word in. "You're sort of right. Jason didn't work out." I relayed the whole story to her as we drank our mochas and laughed at my calamities.

"Trust you to chuck up on the plane in front of him," she said as she howled with laughter. "That Jason sounds like a right prick."

"He was." I smiled and finished the last of my drink. "My turn. I see a change Bev. There's something about you, a glow, a new dress. You've lost your leggings." She went to talk. "Stop, it's still my turn. You always look good so change is hard to detect in that department." Beverley grinned in her own special way and then sipped her drink, awaiting my conclusion. I leaned in and inhaled. "Bev is wearing a new perfume. I suspect Bev is getting something in the love or lust department too." She didn't flinch, giving nothing away. "I suspect lust." She dipped her finger in the froth around the top of her cup and flicked it at me. The milky sludge landed on my nose. I burst into laughter and she joined in. "I'm right aren't I?" She pursed her lips and looked away. "Not the young man who was sitting behind me when we met up last? Beverley Jackson, you big flirt, you didn't?" She was silent. "You did." She emitted that dirty little snigger. I knew it, I'd sussed her out.

"When you left, we exchanged numbers. We haven't been able to keep our hands off each other. I frankly don't care where it's leading but he's too good to turn down. He's good every time, if you get my meaning."

"You're something special, you know that?" I said as I wiped the remains of the sludge off my nose.

We chatted for another hour before she left. I ordered another drink, just a black coffee this time and I relaxed while watching the world go by. A couple holding hands walked past. The man kissed her on the side of the head as they continued along the path. She smiled, then turned and kissed him on the lips. I almost wanted to cry. I have the chance to enjoy what they're experiencing, a second chance at love. Love? Was I in love? It's far too early to say and my hormones are bouncing all over the place. I'm slightly hormonal anyway. Meeting Gavin has just added to my inner chaos, but in a good way. One minute my heart is racing with expectation, another minute, my head is telling me to chill out and take things as they come, and to not be disappointed if things don't go as expected. My heart was winning the battle. I had a good feeling about everything but only time would tell if my instincts were correct. Now, I'm going to take the steaks home, make myself look as good as possible, make the meringue, tidy the bedroom and wait for my man to arrive. That's a huge list of jobs. Bloody hell, is that the time? I grabbed my bag and headed home.

Was he the one?

I pour another glass of red. Yes, you heard right. The plane incident put me off red for a few weeks but with Gavin's encouragement, I gave it another chance and presto, I can keep the stuff down. I'm the luckiest woman in the world. I'm sitting in the beautiful landscaped garden of the Shropshire escape, watching the girls jump in and out of the huge paddling pool. Okay, they didn't get another swimming pool but they got a long stretch of grass, the land beyond and the woodland that backs onto the end of the garden. We have a little dog called Minnie, named after Minnie Mouse. She bounces through the woodland with the girls, yapping as she chases them.

As you can tell, my life has changed dramatically over the past year. I still have my house, or should I say our house. Gavin lives with me and we stay at Shropshire every weekend. We're planning to relocate in several years and live here permanently. I can't wait, Gavin really has built a dream home. He says his dream home is complete because he has me in it. He really does melt my heart. What was once my wardrobe is now half Gavin's. His toothbrush sits next to mine in the holder. My house is his, his Shropshire retreat is mine. I've never been so in love. Sounds cheesy I know but I can't help but share the fact. Did I say I can swim twenty lengths now? In fact, I'm feeling generally fitter thanks to Gavin and his love of swimming.

Gavin gets on really well with the girls. I couldn't ask for more. We have our moments like anyone else who has children. The girls make a mess, Gavin trips over the toys, they don't always want to go to bed on time and they occasionally play up, but all is normal. We laugh our way through life's challenges together.

Andy and Angela are expecting their first child and Gavin is getting used to the thought of being called Grandad. Mallory had a baby boy. She never did balloon in the third trimester. She had this cute little bump that everyone complimented. The girls love Dillon, their new baby brother, and they love spending most of the school holidays with them. Beverley, she's another story. The younger guy moved on soon after but there have been a few since. Beverley hasn't changed and she's still happy, which is all that matters. She still balances the books and manages just about everything at the school, I still teach the children. I still have the cardies. Why would I get rid of them? The children love them. I even get called Ms Cardy by some of them. I may not get called Ms Cardy for long. We've set a date and I can't wait. I know that rhymed but, whatever. My life is the best. Good things can happen out of bad. Life can take the most unexpected turns and I am in love, totally.

"Barbecues on," Gavin said as he leaned down in his apron and kissed me on the forehead. He still makes me tingle. He smiles and winks. We both know that the real magic will happen once the girls have gone to bed, but for now we're having sausages. As he passed, he dropped an envelope in my lap. I go to ask him what it is but he's already walking back towards the barbecue. I open it and pull out a piece of paper. A holiday booking printout. We were all going to Marmaris for a week and get this, he'd rented a villa. No Bates Motel. I jump off the deckchair and run over to him.

"I love you," I said as I flung my arms around him and kissed him.

"I love you too," he replied as he hugged me.

And I did love him, more than anything. Our chance meeting in the airport was the beginning of my new chapter. Meet me at Marmaris Castle, nine years from now, seven in the evening, not a chance!

THE END

Other books by Carla Kovach

Whispers Beneath the Pines
To Let
Flame

25374052R00066

Printed in Poland
by Amazon Fulfillment
Poland Sp. z o.o., Wrocław